CW00863997

New Age Lamians

New Age Lamians

Didi Oviatt

This story is dedicated to my toddler Cannon. May your imagination lead you on great adventures.
Mommy loves you!

One

The story is told in different measures and in different context all over the world. Every family, generation, and village have a different view and belief. There's a myth told by many that the lightning was brought about by the accent Gods, specifically to awaken the Lamians. It's told, that all the magic in life has been stored deep in the tallest mountains of the world for centuries. Mankind once believed that the apocalypse would come by rain of fire. They believed that it would be a great war of nuclear destruction brought upon themselves.

In no way was the world prepared for the real destruction that was to come. And in no way were they ready for the new age. The age of Lamia. However the Lamians came about, and for whatever reason, will forever remain a mystery. A different myth for every walk of the world. All that I believe in are the facts. The origin of the Lamians make no difference to me. I care that they're evil in its truest form, slithering the earth, and that it's my duty to kill them... every last one.

Before the second phase of humanities downfall, that of Lamia, came the first phase, the war of man and nature. The destruction began in the form of fire, but not the sort that was expected. There were no nuclear explosions or dominating nations. The war was one of bone crushing flashes of power raining down from the sky. The lightning began about 50 years before I was born, and it's still crashing into the Earth's surface on a nightly basis, I'm now 26. The first wave of lightning devastated human kind. It destroyed the greatest and smallest of cities alike. Birds fell from the sky and fish floated to the tops of water bodies by the hundreds. Homes burnt to the ground in every direction, and people fell to their deaths. With each almighty strike came unmeasurable devastation.

During the day, people would bury their loved ones and attempt to find food. At night came death and terror in the form of simultaneous lightning storms across the land. Electricity was completely knocked out, causing nothing but sparks and fire in the once booming streets. Jobs became nonexistent causing currency to be rendered meaningless.

The world became every man for himself in a fight for survival. Families came together in small groups to flee from cities and into the mountains and deserts to fend for themselves. Lightning seemed to be stronger and thicker in cities. Roads and power lines acted as beacons, drawing in the crashes from above.

In the first phase, there was one company, and one alone, who survived the electrical apocalypse. The preexisting source that powered this company was invented a mere five years before the lightning began. This company used a wireless energy that was harnessed underground in a liquid form. It sat beneath the sand in three overwhelmingly large locations across the globe. The great phenomenon sent from the heavens seemed to power the company in every sense. The liquid would receive a giant surge of cognition with every strike.

The lights in their facilities burned brighter, their electronics ran faster and more powerful, all systems ran without fail. At first, men and woman were welcomed into the safety of the company's walls. Eventually, their buildings became too crowded and food became sparse. After a few short months of welcoming drifters by the dozens, the company closed its doors. Locks were secured, and gunmen were set in place to take out anyone who became hostile upon the refusal of entrance. Over time, the company grew from a few large buildings, into small cities within giant stone walls. A new flourishing world inside of an old diminishing one. The second phase did not come for years later.

Mankind on the outside have slowly been dying off, while the company has grown stronger and stronger. Time has allowed the remaining people in the world to adapt, and a permanent lifestyle to form. The company no longer bears the name of its owner but is known solely as The Company, for that is all that's needed.

When it all started, my father and I were living in solidarity in a cave deep in the woods. There was a marketplace one mile away where several families met in the afternoon sun, every seventh day. Other families lived in surrounding caves much like ours. We were all very spaced out and far between. This eliminated the possibility of mass destruction with one strike.

At night when the lightning hit we would pray that we wouldn't be the next to fall, or that a forest fire was not sparked nearby. During the day we'd hunt, tend to crops, and fish for whatever remained in a nearby stream. There was no such thing as summer or winter. It was as if time was floating around in a gloomy haze, and we were all stuck in the eye of the storm.

Once every couple of months a care package was dropped into the marketplace by a hovercraft sporting the mark of The Company. The packages contained rare foods, clothes, blankets, and deeply appreciated medicine kits. It was assumed that The Company made the same drops to all known existing communities. The crafts never touched ground unless they were in the safety of The Company walls.

I remember in distinct detail the first time I heard word of the Lamians. I can still picture every detail of the drifter carrying the discarded scales of the beast. My father and I had taken the short hike into the marketplace to mingle with the townsfolk, or so we called them, and to trade hides amongst other hunters. It wasn't much of a marketplace. It was more like a large clearing of grass with blankets laid out to help display items for trade. As we made our way into the clearing, a stirring amongst the crowd became instantly apparent. I glanced at my father in wonder.

"What do you think is going on?"

"It's hard to say, but there's a man down there that I've never seen before."

"Another drifter you suppose? It's been a while since we've seen a new face."

I remember my father's expression being stern and unreadable as he replied, "Stay close to me, Son. You remember the last drifter was out for blood. We mean nothing to them, they only want our food and supplies. Stay close at all times."

We back tracked slowly into the trees unnoticed. We stashed the few rabbits and fish we had intended on trading. There was no need to bring them into the clearing to be taken. We were not to risk being killed by some stranger passing through for a short meal.

After covering our leather packs of goods with dirt and sticks, we returned to the edge of the clearing empty handed. My father and I walked shoulder to shoulder into the small group that formed in the center of the marketplace. This drifter was the biggest and dirtiest man I had ever seen. He stood a full foot above me and I prided myself on being the tallest in my spaced-out village. Laying at his feet was a huge shedding of what had to be some sort of a serpent's skin.

I'd only seen a few snakes in my lifetime and they were nothing in comparison to this. He had it rolled up into a giant ball that sat on the ground, reaching up to his waist. The man stood next to old Mr. Hawthorn, who had joined our community when I was a small boy. Neither of them said a word. They stood side by side, waiting for the entire crowd to gather before speaking. Our marketplace gatherings were usually small. We were lucky to have twenty or so people trudge the unwelcoming walks from their caves. Some had to travel for miles to make their exchanges, so they skipped more than they attended.

I nodded at Mr. Hawthorn in welcome as he glanced in my direction. He dropped his head quickly to his chest in return, then he spoke in a loud voice, enunciating practically every word.

"I guess there is enough of us here. Johnson has a story to share with you all."

He looked up at the drifter. Their eyes met in a disturbing silence before the drifter broke the glance and picked up the shedding.

"As this kind man mentioned, my name is Johnson. I'm from very far away and have been traveling for several years. I've seen many things that no man should see. I've witnessed the good, and evil of The Company. I've lived to experience the life of predator and prey. I'll answer every question you have for me, but first I must show you this. You all must understand that there's something out there. Something that's inevitably coming your way. You cannot stop it, and you cannot hide from it. It's the bringer of death and is far more powerful than God's weapon raining down at night. I've heard several stories of this beast in my travels, but until about a year ago I was oblivious to its reality."

I studied the drifters face as I listened to his words. He was obviously aged by the sun and weather. His skin was like leather, with eyes covered in wrinkles, and a chin blanketed with hair. His beard touched down to his mid neckline and moved as he spoke. I listened to the scratch in his voice and watched the slight shake in his hands. I wondered how old this man must have been.

He spoke with a certain confidence and truth in his voice. With his arms wrapped around the rolled-up snake's skin, he left the crowd making his way to the tree line. Bending at the waist, he unraveled the discarded skin. I watched as this towering man unrolled the ball. He left one end at edge of the grass, and slowly rolled the rest through the waiting crowd, to the other end of the clearing. The rolling ball grew smaller and smaller as the laid-out portion was left behind in one long, thick, impossible looking group of scales, stretching out across the entire length of the clearing. Shock instilled into the voices of the men and women standing next to me. I on the other hand, stood speechless along with my silent father.

The dead and detached skin of this snake stretched along the entire distance of the clearing that we'd proclaimed as the marketplace. Each scale was larger in diameter than the length of my wrist to forearm. Fearful whispers lingered in the crowd.

"Where did you come across this snake skin?" ask my father.

"It's been passed through two other travelers before me, along with the story of its origins. But I assure you, Sir, this is the skin of no snake."

"It looks like a snake to me."

"At first glance, yes," he replied. "But, notice the shape. It doesn't shrink down on both sides nor have the head of a snake. It triples the size on one end as the other."

Again, my father retorted "That doesn't mean anything. What if it's much larger and just broken in the middle?"

Rolling laughter escaped from the drifter's lips.

"I do like your style my good sir! Come along with me to the end, and I'll show you something before I tell you all the tale of what this skin belongs to."

My father walked next to the drifter and I followed close in tow. The rest of the crowd slowly made their way behind us, at an understandably cautious distance. I stared down at the skin laying at my feet as I made step after step to the edge of the clearing. The skin grew wider and wider until it came to an abrupt stop.

After pointing at the end of the shedding, Johnson explained the way that the scales shrunk down around the edges of the final row, and they rounded into a different shape. In conclusion, he noted the slight indents at the outer edges indicating the way the scales formed and attached to the creature. Nodding his head, my father seemed to agree with the drifter's logic.

I let my eyes wander the length of the shedding. I was overwhelmed by the size and mystery of it. It was dark gray in color with a blueish tint, unlike the average clear or tan pigment held by most other reptile shedding. Each scale was diamond in shape, aside from that final and largest row. An eerie beauty radiated from it, as its flow filled the grassy clearing and demanded the attention of every man and woman standing close.

"You do have my attention, Mr. Johnson."

"Just Johnson, please." He requested with a warm smile. "They're calling these creatures Lamians. Half serpent, half man. Well... woman, I should say."

Already a head taller than the rest, he seemed to stand even higher. His proud smile quickly faded into a menacing stare into the distance. A cloud crossed over the wrinkles on his face and the bags under his eyes.

"Upon much study, the story has been passed along with the skin. After seeing the terror in the eyes of a few men and women before I came across it, I believe every word. It's said that snakes carrying the Lamian venom were stirred awake from an ancient sleep. The shock of the lightning, and the horrendous roll of the omnipotent thunder, unleashed its power. Snakes containing the most potent of a magical blood-line awoke from centuries of undisturbed slumber."

I nodded, following the lead of my father, and we crossed our arms over our chests.

"The original beast was said to be transformed from a human into a serpent hundreds of thousands of years ago. She had an overwhelming loss in her life. She denounced the Gods, and in turn was cursed herself to live out her life as a serpent. Her name was Lamia. Upon being slaughtered by humans, the unborn snakes inside of her was put to rest by the Gods. That is... until the lightning began. The storm awoke the decedent snakes of Lamia. Her blood boiled in their veins. Her sight peered through their eyes, seeking out only the most beautiful women alive to carry out her plan of mayhem."

Johnson drew in a lungful of air, lowered his chin, and looked around at our faces, lowering his voice as he spoke further. We as a crowd was silent.

"Upon finding these women, the snakes would sink their fangs deep into the flesh, infecting them with Lamia's poisonous venom. It's said that this venom forever changed the women bitten. At first their beauty lasted for years, not allowing them to age. As time went on, the serpent inside of them started to surface changing them into awful creatures, harboring the revenge against humans that Lamia herself harbored. They now feed off the blood and flesh of humans, sucking them dry in seconds. Once a serpent's venom has completely taken over a woman, the evil that is their new selves devour their old souls. They move from house, to hut, and to cave, consuming every human they meet. They travel and feed at night, amongst the lightning, when the rest of the world is in hiding."

Glancing around at the faces in the crowd Johnson's expression remained the same as it had when he began his tale. He explained that he had made it his mission to travel as far and as fast as he could to warn survivors of the storm, that the Lamians are coming. He didn't know how far away this skin was picked up, or how fast the creatures moved. He also stated that it had been at least a year since he had been to a place that already heard of the beasts.

I looked up and down the length of the clearing at the giant shed skin of the serpent as he spoke. No matter how hard I imagined, I just couldn't picture this horrendous being. My stomach twisted and stirred at the thought. I was only twenty-two years old at the time, with no life experience other than that of our cave and the marketplace. I'm now twenty-six, and my story has changed to one of courage, and heartbreak.

The following week went by quickly. Mr. Hawthorn insisted that Johnson stay with him until the following week's gathering. He was certain that The Company would be making a drop and that his towering new friend could use the supplies provided in his travels. Hawthorn had been timing the drop for years. If they didn't hover within the first couple days of Johnson's arrival, then they'd surely show up within the following seven after that.

My father and I stayed as busy as possible that week, trying to keep our minds occupied. Hunting more than usual didn't quite pay off as well as we were hoping for, but we did have a few larger meals than what we were used to. Sleep was rudely interrupted with dreams of strange creatures and serpents making their way into our cave. The seventh day couldn't come fast enough, at least not for me. My father was a different story. He refused to speak of the drifter, insisting that the man was as crazy as every other traveler. Of course, his eyes and facial expressions didn't match the words he spoke.

Though my father remained as calm and collected as he was every other day, he still seemed to be up and ready for our trip to the marketplace a bit earlier than usual. I remember this day to be the biggest and most important of my life, second only to the day of my injection. The seventh day since our last marketplace journey had finally rolled around. Not only were we expecting a drop from The Company, but I'd also be able to hear more stories from the strange man with a skin of the Lamian.

My father's moccasins were secured to his feet, and his trading bag was fastened around his waist before I was even out of bed. I jumped quickly to my feet, splashed a little water on my face and threw some jerky in my pocket to snack on during the walk. A mile's journey seemed much longer than it had every other week, even though we made it in record time.

Thinking we would be amongst the first to arrive had proved to be a silly assumption. The clearing was full of every man, woman, and child within a ten-mile range. Faces that were rare to the marketplace had emerged from every cave and dugout around. Apparently, news had traveled fast of the man with the proof of a living monster.

They'd all come to see the serpent shedding and to hear Johnson's stories. The soft sound of a hovercraft soon hummed from miles away. Cheers came from the mouths and hands of everyone surrounding me. I recall the excitement along with the look of anxiety in my father's eyes. He didn't clap or whoop or holler. He stood stiff and in fear. It was as if he could smell the terror that was coming.

I looked up into the sky as the hovercraft came into view, expecting a parachuted bag to drop out of the bottom. No parachutes were ejected. The craft dropped down and slowly lowered itself toward the ground. Directly above our heads and into the clearing, it came closer and closer. Panic quickly surged through the crowd.

"They're going to land right on us!" An elderly woman shouted.

We ran in every direction, scattering like bugs from beneath an upturned log or boulder. My father held onto my arm as we ran out of the marketplace and back into the safety of the trees.

The hovercrafts took up nearly the entire grassy clearing, there were three. A door lifted from the first, allowing a few men to step out. They were dressed in strange black suits. The first man to emerge from the craft held a large cone up to his mouth and shouted into it. His voice rang through the woods with power.

"Please don't run. We're here to help you. We're here to talk to you and give you supplies in person." He called.

I looked at my father in question as we hid behind a large rock concealing us from the craft. He peeked from around it as a small group slowly made their way back to the men in suits. He motioned with his hand for me to look. I watched as the men from The Company handed out bread and new clothing. My father took in a deep breath of defeat and whispered to me.

"They've been helping us for years. I think if they wanted to hurt us they could have done it a thousand times over by now."

"Do you think we should go talk to them?" I asked quietly.

"Yes, Son, but be cautious."

I followed my father toward the strange men, hesitation was heavy in my steps. Behind us walked Mr. Hawthorn and Johnson. Johnson had left the serpent shedding in the trees. I assumed that he wanted to hide it from our unexpected guests. I recalled him saying that he'd seen the good and bad in The Company, and I observed the caution in his movements.

At first there were ten of the suited men, mingling kindly with the men and women from our so-called village. They asked us questions about our lifestyle but kept any information regarding The Companies' growth and intentions to themselves. Every time the slightest mention of Johnson's serpent possession started to come up he'd jump in the conversation and change the subject. My father and I along with Mr. Hawthorn noticed his scramble for silence.

We each took our part in helping him keep the secret. Ultimately, the truth of Johnson's presence was kept under wraps. It was apparent that the technology produced from The Company had advanced tenfold from that of the stories my father had told me. They could create more than any regular cave dweller, like myself, could dream as reality.

After a couple hours of gift giving and meaningless chatter, the man with the megaphone stepped up again to address the people.

"Can I have your attention, please?" He waited for silence before continuing. "Thank you, kind folks for allowing us to crash in on your gathering, it's been enjoyable. As you know, The Company has been giving medicine and treatments for illnesses to the common people. I must ask you now to help us in return. There are tests to be ran, and studies to be performed, to make any advancements in the medical field. All that I ask for is a simple blood sample from each of you. It'll be a tiny prick on the arm and then we must be on our way. I assure you it's painless."

A quick bond of trust had formed among the people of my village and the people of The Company. We agreed to the man's request and lined up willingly for their blood tests to commence. I watched as Johnson stood to the back of the crowd. He waited as close as he could get to the tree line without being noticed. I squeezed my father's arm getting his attention and nudged him with my shoulder toward Johnson. We followed Johnson's lead and waited for our turn in the very back of the line.

The men and women held their breath, or squinted their eyes, and the children let out small squeals as The Company took their blood samples. I leaned in and listened closely as my father whispered a quick conversation back and for with Johnson.

"Why do you think they would need our blood for medical advancements? Can't they test on each other?"

"They're probably looking for a tie, with us and the Lamians. That'd be my guess, but it is hard to say." Johnson whispered back so quietly that I could hardly hear his answer.

"You said that when a woman is bitten, it takes years for her to change, right?"

"Yes."

"Do you think The Company knows about this serpent you speak of? Do you think they could be looking for them in the human form?"

"Oh, trust me they know. The Company knows everything that goes on. They're the only ones who do, and they've been hiding it from you and everyone else all this time. I don't trust them, not one bit."

My father was quiet after that. He waited for his turn in silence as we inched our way closer and closer to the men in strange suits. I watched my father stare into the man's eyes as he held out his arm without a flinch. Next it was my turn. I looked back and forth at the two men performing my test. One held out a black box with a hole in the center for my arm to slide into. The other held a small screen and watched as a string of numbers ran across the center of it in a bright purple light.

I'd never seen anything like it. My father had told me of the wonders of technology, but so far all I'd ever seen was the glowing colors on the bottom of The Companies hover crafts. I slid my arm into the box. A sudden pinch burned into my skin. I pulled my arm back out and watched as the man holding the small screen gasped.

"He has it!" The man said quietly and with much excitement to his partner. "Bill, get over here with that other tester."

He yelled to another man in a suit that was standing closer to the craft. This second man pulled a matching screen out of a small pack that was hanging loosely from his shoulder. He touched the screen onto the top of the black metal box and informed me to slide my arm back in. I looked back and forth between Johnson and my father.

"Go ahead, Son."

My father reluctantly answered my unspoken question. He stood closer to my side and stared at the screen being held by this new man with a new tester. I slid my arm back into the box and again felt a slight pinch. This time seemed a bit more painful than the first.

"Oh my, you're right."

All the men in suits suddenly swarmed around me.

"What? I have What?" I demanded.

There was no answer to my question, only a sudden confusion amongst them. More men in matching suits began to pile out of the hovercrafts, carrying strange fire arms. My father told me stories of guns and bombs of every shape and size, but until that day I'd never seen any. Quickly forming a small circle around me, the men pushed me toward the craft. This was the first real feeling of panic I'd ever experienced.

"Father!" I yelled. I pushed against the men, but they were like a wall, separating me from my frightened dad. "What are you doing?!?" I shouted at them. "Let me go!"

I reached over their shoulders, stretching my hand toward my father who, along with Johnson was trying to reach me. They tried with no avail to fight off the men of The Company. A loud *bang* rang through the air. It sounded much like the thunder of the night crashing around me. The men and women of my beloved community screamed and ran back into the hills. Soon, everyone besides my father and Johnson were gone. As The Company whisked me away from the clearing and into the first hovercraft, my father screamed in my direction.

"Jackson!"

His voice cracking through the commotion and screeching my name, still haunts me to this day. That was the first day of my new life. A life to be spent as the right hand of a Company who stole me away from everything I'd ever known and loved. A life of war and technology twisted and warped into an unexpectedly violent existence. Aside from my oh so realistic dreams of simple and happier times with my father, all that remains now is the memory of him yelling my name in panic.

As I scrambled and reached for my father, I felt a strong and sudden pinch in my shoulder. I looked down to see a strange plastic device pushing fluid into my skin. Pulling away was impossible. My eyes started closing and my muscles relaxed as the doors to the hovercraft closed around me. Everything went instantly dark. I slipped into an awkward, drug induced unconsciousness.

Two

The next three weeks were nothing if not long and irritating. Sleep, eat, run, and answer questions aloud that were asked by a computerized voice coming out of multiple speakers throughout my new home. That was my routine. The day I was taken, I awoke in a strange place full of loneliness and silence. And, every day after was the same, up until the day of my injection.

I later learned that I was in captivity for three weeks, before the horrid day of my injection. Every day I'd awake from a light, unnerved sleep in an uncomfortably oversized living space. I arose out of my bed and slipped on the plain gray sweat suit that had been laid out for me, by whom I didn't know. I was yet to meet a single person from The Company. Well, aside from the small group who had taken me unexpectedly from my village. Since that day I'd remained in solitary confinement.

Every day I was ordered to place a few thin, sticky devices onto my head and chest. I would then have to run on a strange machine, and lift weights while being watched like some sort of experiment through cameras protruding in every corner of my new home. If I refused to follow orders from the voice ringing in, or if I declined to eat every morsel of the food sent in on small trays from a hole in the wall, then I'd be punished. I'd be starved for a full day and declined in my requests for water.

Until one day was different. It was the day of my injection, and it changed everything about who I was. The serum transformed me into who I now am. Everything about me changed into something different. Everything! As I shimmied my legs into the loose-fitting sweatpants that morning, the voice rang in loud and clear.

"Today is the day of your injection." It said. "The door will be unlocked in exactly one hour. You will then be allowed into the halls of The Company. Today presents an enormous privilege for you and for the colleagues around you. Along with privilege, comes a heavy burden. You are not to speak with anyone. You are to stay to your left until you reach a large red door labeled *Third Division Injection Lab*. Enter this door and immediately take a seat in the chairs provided. Do not move from your seated position until you are instructed to do so. Failure to comply in full of The Company's orders, will result in your immediate destruction."

After chomping down every bite of my breakfast, I sat next to the door and waited for it to open. My father had told me of watches and clocks. He'd explained to me what they looked like and about how before the lightning apocalypse, people would use them to tell time. I knew that it was a clock on the wall above my bed, but I didn't have the slightest idea how to use it. What was an hour?

I sat on the floor, waiting for some sort of sound or indication that the door was going to open. I watched the clock on the wall as the hands moved around it. When the door finally opened I quickly stood and followed the directions that were given. I reached my ordered destination and sat in my chair. I stared at the seemingly fresh white paint on the walls and tried to clear my mind. I imagined my father. What was he doing at this very moment?

I knew now that The Company was a force to be reckoned with. I'd follow any orders given to me without question. I wondered what exactly it was that they'd found in my blood. I thought about the giant snake skin and the story told by Johnson. I couldn't think of any instance in my entire life that I'd been bitten by a snake. I also remembered Johnson saying that the Lamians were women. I just knew, without a doubt, that there was no way my blood could have anything to do with the creatures Johnson spoke of.

I recall sitting in the waiting room, full of anticipation on injection day. The tapping of my foot nearly drowned out the irritating clicking noise coming from the mouth of a young man stirring in his seat next to me. Sitting directly in the middle of a row of equally nervous men and women, allowed me to feel the heat of the room and to smell the sweat rapidly accumulating. There were twelve of us awaiting our fate.

The room was small and stuffy. Although the walls were painted white and the windows were large, allowing an ample amount of light in, I could still feel the acuteness of our allotted space. The pupils in my eyes had shrunk in attempt to adjust to the brightness surrounding me. I sat in silence while the orders from the familiar computerized voice bounced around in my head.

There was a large black and orange clock on the wall directly above the door in front of us. I watched again blankly as the hands moved around the circle. I wondered how long we'd been sitting there waiting. I was never a very patient person up until that day. My father would often scorn me for chasing away the game we were hunting, because I couldn't sit still long enough.

I bit my tongue, trying to stop myself from speaking to anyone else in the room. I wondered if they'd been taken the same as me. I craved information of their families and to share the horrors of my father scrambling to reach me. Just as the words formed in my throat and were about to escape from my lips, a short brunette man walked into the room.

He was wearing a white overcoat and holding a clear board. It had a metal clip at the top, with a small stack of pages attached to it. Everything about this man was alien to me. Including the assortment of colored sticks that were jammed into his jacket pocket. I later learned them to be pens. He looked to be in his mid to late 30s. There wasn't so much as a hint of kindness in his eyes or humor in his smile. He looked around at the line of us, sitting there, just waiting for him to speak. An evil grin slowly formed across one side of his face, while the other side remained in place.

"So, this is what they've given me to work with, huh?"

It was a rhetorical question. His voice was low and menacing. Not seeming to fit the man's size. At first glance, I would've pictured him to have a high pitched or whiny voice, but it was neither.

"Which one of you is Jackson Bellony?"

The pit of my stomach dropped to my toes as I shifted in my seat and slowly lifted my hand. The shaking of my fingers must have been noticeable. He observed my surfacing nerves, and rolled his eyes at the sight of me.

"Well, it looks like you're first. Come with me."

It was hard for me to stand up and part from the crowd. Though I didn't actually met any of these people, in a strange way it still felt like I was being pulled away from a comfort zone. For a moment I was a part of a group. I didn't even get to know them, before I was singled out, yet again.

Vulnerability was now setting in as I walked away from the row of chairs and into the unknown on my own. Once again, I was being singled out and for what, I did not know. I turned my head to look back at the tall blonde boy who was sitting next to me clicking his tongue. He was now silent. He watched me walk away with a sigh of relief. Surely, he must've been glad that he wasn't chosen to go first. I imagined my response would've been the same, had it been this boy walking away from me.

As I took my awkward steps toward the man in front of me, he continued to speak to the rest of the room.

"The door behind you is a bathroom. Use it only if you must and then return to your seat. You're to remain silent always. My name is David. I'm a third division assistant. Susana is my collogue, and she'll be coming to take the next of you on the list. We've split you into two teams of six. We will take turns moving you into the lab for your injections. You won't ask questions. You'll wait patiently for your turn and everything will be explained in due time."

David glared up at me from the corner of his eye as I stood next to him. He looked even shorter, now that I was standing so close. David didn't seem to mind looking up at me. I suppose he had to do it his whole life. I wondered briefly if that's why he seemed so grumpy. The thought made me chuckle in mind. It was a futile effort to keeping the mood light. I thought for a moment that drumming up a little humor might help me to control the itching anxiety that was racing through me. It didn't faze it.

My father had always gotten irritated at me when I would tell stupid jokes or try and cheer him up when he was down. This was a day when my stomach churned at the thought of my father. My heart was ready to leap completely out of my chest and run for the hills. I follow David through the door and out of the unsettling white waiting room.

He quickly led the way down a wide stretch of hallway. Having lived in a cave all my life, I was only told stories of houses and buildings, but had never seen the reality of their structure. My father had stacks upon stacks of books that were passed to him from before the storm. He taught me to read and write at a young age, with old books, and with sticks in the sand. He'd insisted on the importance of keeping knowledge alive amongst the simple folk. Reading the books was much of a challenge for me. Most words were meaningless, for I'd never experienced the things they described. This left everything to my imagination, which was overactive and none the helpful. The walls around me were nothing like I'd imagined them to be. The formation of The Company was an amazement all in its own.

We passed a small amount of David's peers, who were all wearing the same white jacket as he. The only noticeable difference that separated David from them was the color of his undershirt and his shoes. Only a fraction of the shirt underneath his white coat was showing but the color was hard to miss. The shade was one I'd never before seen on fabric. The only clothing dropped down to our little marketplace was very plain. I had only seen fabric in shades of browns or grays. Other than that, we all wore leather that we'd stretched, beaten, and tanned ourselves from the hides of animals we hunted.

A very bright lime green undershirt was something I hadn't so much as dreamed of. His shoes looked the same as mine in every way accept for the tread, it too matched the color of his shirt. I could only see it for brief moments at a time as his heel lifted with each step. I walked behind him with my eyes wide and knees weak. I tried as hard as I could to memorize every detail of my surroundings.

The overbearing white in every direction was blinding. I'd never felt so clean or lonely in all my life. The few men and women passing us in the hall looked straight ahead. None of them were so much as glancing in my direction. I screamed on the inside for acknowledgment and human contact. Each one passed by with a purpose, and were seemingly in a hurry.

One woman passed with the collar of her undershirt showing as well. I couldn't help but to turn my head and follow her with my eyes, admiring the vivid color. The most beautiful shade of pink I had ever seen was protruding out from underneath her white collard jacket. Just as I suspected, the underpart of her shoes matched her shirt in the same fashion as David's. I wondered briefly why they had so far been the only two with this distinction, but the thought faded quickly. I had too much on my mind to worry to deeply about such details.

What is this injection? My fate was an unsettling mystery. My entire life had been pulled away from me, suddenly and painfully. Only three prior, I was ripped away from my father. The same feeling from that day was again re-signing in my chest. Like a broken chunk of concrete there was a solid, heavy, unmovable weight sitting between my ribs.

The hallway was mostly blank, with only a few doors in sight. They were each coded with numbers only. The lack of explanation as to what was lurking behind each door, was making the short walk that much more antagonizing. The lights flickered above our heads as David finally made a stop next to the first door to contain a little color on the number tag. Of course, it was the same lime green that was on his shirt and shoes.

Glancing over the top of him at the next door down, I noticed the pink number tag matching that of the woman's we passed in the hall. I assumed that woman must have been the Susana girl David had mentioned, but I dare not ask. David looked me up and down for a moment then spoke in a strange low tone.

"There's no way to explain or prepare you for what's to happen in your future. But I can tell you this… once you cross through this door, your life will never be the same. What you make of the injection given to you today is entirely up to you. What is meant to happen with you has the potential for an utter failure or a completely epic game changer for the entire world. I want you to know before you meet your doctor that I'm routing for you."

The hatred in David's glare seemed to melt away into a shortly lived compassion. Holding out his hand in a kind gesture was unexpected. I slowly took his palm into mine and gave it a quick shake. The kindness in David's face abruptly hardened. In the blink of an eye the original angry shell that was David had returned.

"You will stay directly behind me with your head down. You will not make eye contact with any of the men or women behind this door. I will lead you directly to your doctor and at that point you will be allowed to speak. Do you understand?"

My response was a simple, "yes."

I understood my instructions loud and clear. Curiosity had taken a hold of me to say the least. The brick in my chest was slowly dissolving, but the debris it left behind clung to everything that the main chunk of it had once touched. My ribs were left forever weighted. Completely epic game changer? I'm routing for you? What does this strange little man mean by all of this?

My fears were rapidly changing into adrenaline. I dropped my head to the floor and stared at David's feet. As the door silently swung open the noise of the crowd behind it rose. There must've been dozens of people rushing back and forth. I dare not look up to make a head count. I followed closely behind David as he quickly led me through the bunch of company workers. Like busy builder bees, they kept their hive running. Noisily, they swarmed and buzzed on either side of me.

I noticed the feet of those around me as we sped across the floor. Lime green flashes were everywhere. The open space must have been bigger than I expected, because the walk within the hustle and bustle of the working Company men was much longer than that of the hallway.

David stopped abruptly. I nearly plowed into the back of him as my concentration on his movements were delayed. The fog in my head was becoming thicker and thicker as I was trying to listen to the commotion. I'd never heard so many voices all in the same place at once. I longed for the silence of the woods and the comfort of my cave. I felt as if I was stripped naked to be paraded around in front of a million strangers. David promptly swung open another door and I followed in behind him. He slammed the door closed, shutting off the noise like the snap of a finger. Silence again filled my ears. I glanced at David from the tops of my eyes through a bowed head. He nodded his own in response indicating me to look forward. I raised my head slowly to meet the eyes of the most beautiful woman I'd ever seen. Her mouth instantly spread across her face into a perfect grin.

"Jackson!! I'm so excited to finally meet you!" Her face was warm, and her voice alluring. "Please, please, take a seat."

She pointed to a black thinly-cushioned chair. An unexpected flutter in my stomach moved through me as she spoke. Even the scent of her was intoxicating. I took the seat without question and stared at her while she explained.

"I'm Brooklyn, your doctor. I will be preforming the injection and overseeing your treatment over the next few weeks until you move into the knowledge and training phase." Sitting directly across from me in a matching chair, she stared kindly into my eyes. "I must say Jackson, to find a young man with the G-Factor, at such a perfect age, and in such immaculate health, is a real excitement around here. The serum has been ready for five whole years now, and the need of people to inject has taken a sudden turn from experiment to necessity. You, Jackson, could be everything we've been looking for!"

The excitement was illuminating around Dr. Brooklyn. Concentration was hard as I was unable to look away from her giant green eyes. She seemed to be waiting on a response, but my words caught in my throat. I wasn't even sure where to start. The questions I had for her were piling up in my head, yet for some reason I couldn't seem to spit any them out. The first words I spoke to Dr. Brooklyn were simply stammered.

"Puh, Puh, Please, ma'am, call me Jack."

"Jack!... I love it!" She squealed in response and continued, "I'm not going to lie to you, Jack, the injection will be painful. This is not going to be an easy day for you. But of course, you can't expect a raw string of liquid technology coursing through every fiber of your body to be painless right!?!"

"Rah, Rah, what?"

"Oh Jack, we have SO much to talk about. But I'm afraid time is not a luxury within our grasp. We must go over things quickly and get the ball rolling. But, trust me, in a couple of days when you're back on your feet we will have all the time needed to go over everything."

"What do you mean back on my feet? What is the G-Factor? And what do you mean technology in my body?" I was starting to get angry as the fog in my mind thickened. I didn't have a clue what she was talking about. Everything she said was streaming together and cutting in and out. "What exactly are you going to be injecting?" I managed to spit out the simple yet extremely complex question that had been swarming through me since I heard the voice announce the words injection day that morning.

Dr. Brooklyn glanced down at the sheets of papers on her lap, and quickly thumbed through a couple pages before she looked back up at me.

"I can see here that you're much more knowledgeable than the other cave dwellers we've meet. You can read, you have some basic math skill, and your vocabulary is very well disciplined. You shouldn't have a hard time at all understanding what I'm about to explain to you." She slowed her words and her excitement faded into utter seriousness. "There is a monster among us Jackson. We as The Company must fight this beast from within the safety of our walls, as to secure our preservation. We've been unable to defeat this creature with chemical warfare, and they move through our fire power as if they were never touched. We're going to have to fight in person. We've created a serum that can flow through the veins of a human, attaching microfibers throughout the cells. We've been testing on mice and pigs for years, and so far, this serum has killed off every host injected aside from those containing the G-Factor, as we call it. It's an extra, and very unique chromosomal link. You, Jack, have this Factor. You should have no trouble surviving the serum. After you're injected we'll be able to see what you are seeing and hear what you are hearing. If there is breath in your lungs and beat in your heart, we will know your exact location and every detail of your surroundings. You'll become the eyes and ears of The Company in human form."

Her voice became quicker and higher in pitch as she spoke. The excitement returned slowly, and by the time she was finished with the speech, Dr. Brooklyn was nearly bouncing out of her seat.

"This is all not to mention the fact that your muscles will change and progress at a rapid pace. You will be stronger, smarter, faster, and more resilient in every way!" Dr. Brooklyn's smile spread widely across her face.

I sat in shock. "What if I don't want this *injection*? Don't I have a say in any of this?"

Thinking back now, I'm sure that I didn't fully understand the responsibilities to come. I was neither excited nor scared, as much as I was lost. I was completely and utterly lost inside myself. I was a mere child, naive to the world I was living in. Oblivious to my own possibilities.

"Well Jack, I'm sorry to inform you that you do not have a choice. You see…" She stopped and pointed up to the camera in the corner of the room. I glanced up, staring at it as I listened to her finish. "The Company is watching you now, and they care little about your small life before coming here. To the men on the other side of that camera you're nothing but a tool. If you do not come with me willingly, then you'll be forced. If you do not comply, and follow orders after your injection, then you'll be destroyed without the batting of an eye." She sighed and looked to her feet. "I'm sorry that it has to be this way Jack, but you have to understand that you cannot change things. The Company is what it is, and it's vital to our existence as a human race."

She raised her head back up, her eyes meeting mine. I didn't know what to say. I was stunned by her willing acceptance of The Companies standards, guidelines and rules. A mere hint of pity or compassion, I wasn't sure which, clouded over the excitement in her eyes. We held our gaze only for a few short moments before the clearing of David's throat cut through the air like a serrated knife. I'd nearly forgotten he was in the room. I'd been so engrossed in Dr. Brooklyn and the contents of her speech that everything around me faded away. After breaking the silent moment between the doctor and I, David insisted that we move into the injection room. Dr. Brooklyn agreed after looking down at her watch first and then back up to the two of us.

"Well, Jack, follow me." Her words had a proficient edge. As would the blade of a knife, it cut to my core.

"Keep your head down, like before." David demanded.

I walked between the two of them with my head down. My eyes followed the green soles of the attractive doctor's feet. The walk was a blur. I no longer listened to the rushed voices around me. I didn't bat an eye at the people scurrying from one side of me to the other. I didn't care about their jobs or their purpose of The Company. Not so much as a passing whisper caught my attention.

Everything that Dr. Brooklyn told me about this injection was rolling around my brain like loose pebbles. I tried to make sense of what was about to happen. I imagined these microscopic fibers attaching themselves to me. The picture was impossible to paint, and despite the clear description given, I hadn't a clue what was coming. The thud of my heartbeat rang too loudly in my ears to concentrate on anything but the shaking in my hands and weakness in my knees.

I wondered how much stronger I could possibly get, imagining myself with bulging arms and rippling pecks. As hard as I tried, I couldn't picture it. I thought about all the animals that died after the injection. Would I even wake up from this catastrophe? Is today my last day? I wondered. My lips parted only a crack to fill my lungs with the muggy over populated air. I felt like I was going to pass out before we even reached this injection lab they spoke of.

Dr. Brooklyn abruptly stopped at a solid metal door and turned to face me.

"Now Jack, I know you're scared, but I assure you everything is for the greater good, and will turn out just fine in the long run. I'm going to need you to do everything I tell you to without question. You'll be restrained, and it is for your own good. Please do not fight it, Jack. That could be a very large and painful mistake on your part."

I stared at her wide eyed and cautious. She leaned in and gave me a quick but unforgettable kiss on the cheek before shoving the door open. My eyes wandered from one end of the room to the other. I'm not sure exactly what I expected, but I do know that this wasn't it. The center of the room contained a large see through tank, full to the brim with some dirty looking liquid. Surrounding it, was screen after screen of large flat table-style machines that I later learned to be computers. Each with a person standing next to it. I instantly recognized the fact that they'd been waiting for me. Dr. Brooklyn pointed around the room at all the people.

"Each of these men and women have a special purpose. They'll be assisting me in your transformation."

As she spoke, two men walked up to me and started stripping me of the comfort of my gray sweat-suit. My muscles clenched, and I flinched in embarrassment, yet I willed myself to remain silent. No one besides my father had seen me naked, and even when I changed in front of him he would look away. Not since I was a baby being dressed by my mother, had I been in the buff around a woman. She passed away when I was 5, God rest her soul. I looked down in shame, remembering the warning not to fight. I wanted more than anything to grab my clothes and run, but not before knocking a few of these company wimps to the ground. I held in the notion and wearily looked back up at Dr. Brooklyn.

She explained to me that I'd be lowered into the liquid. She told me to breath just the same once I was emerged, just as I do on a regular basis. As she voiced the instructions, the same two men who had stripped me of my clothes, fastened tight plastic cuffs around my wrists, ankles, and waist. The cuffs were secured to a couple of bars at my sides and above my head by thin yet obviously indestructible cables. Before I knew it, I was being hoisted up into the air.

The metal bars were strong, holding me in place with my feet shoulder width apart, and my arms extending out to my sides. The doctor no longer made any explanations. She turned her back to me and started spitting out orders to the rest of the room. I watched from above, as the distance between myself and the floor exceeded.

I was lowered into the tank feet first. The liquid was a thick, warm gel. I wiggled my toes feeling the slime slip and then mold into place between them. By the time I was waist deep I could no longer move my feet. I became motionless and without feeling as I descended to my fate. Further and further down I was engulfed in the shocking warm fluid. Past my stomach and to my neck.

I took in shallow breathes as the icy gel touched my chin. Leaning my head back, I tried to keep my mouth out for as long as I could. The wetness engulfed the remainder of my flesh entirely. I held my breath and opened my eyes. Everything was a blur. I could see the silhouette of each body in the room, yet I couldn't tell apart who was man and who was woman.

I peered out of the tank in fear, searching for Dr. Brooklyn, but with no success. I remembered her words to breath the liquid as if I was breathing regular air. I was completely motionless from head to toe. I couldn't feel a thing aside from the weakening pound of my heart. The lack of oxygen was dulling my mind as I continued to hold my breath. After a few more seconds, I could no longer take it. I felt as if my chest was going to explode leaving my body dead in this disgusting paralyzing gel.

I couldn't take it any longer. Unable to part my lips, I let the air out through my nostrils and took in a giant sniff. Rather than air filling my lungs, I felt the slime make its way down my nasal cavity and into my chest. Strangely, I felt as if I'd been breathing it all my life. Oxygen was flowing through my body and into my brain as if I was breathing the natural fresh air I'd taken for granted on an otherwise normal day.

No sooner than my body began to relax the pain struck. The first needles were injected into the backs of my knees. I could feel each one, long and sharp as they pushed through my skin and into the joints of my legs. I tried with all my strength to move away from the sting, but I was rendered motionless. The molded gel held me in place as the same pain was now being shoved into the insides of my elbows. Followed by my neck and lower back. I tried to move away and escape the torture, but I couldn't. The mold held me in place as all six needles made their way further and further, painfully into my flesh.

The excruciating shock of the serum was then pushed into my body though these multiple burning needle tips. It was thick, like hardening sap on a pine tree. I felt it burn its way into my veins. Engulfing my body in a burning inferno. Every molecule hurt as the fibers attached themselves throughout me. It spread like a slow-moving plague, infecting my body with smoldering hot lava.

Though motionless on the outside, I was screaming and thrashing on the inside. With every beat of my heart the burning pressure was pushed from one end of my body to the other, reaching my brain very last. I felt as if my head was exploding into a thousand pieces. Like it was being ripped apart by rabid wolves. I screamed at the top of my lungs, yet was heard by no one, as the sound was masked by the disgustingly thick gel I was being held in. My mind darkened. It clouded over by a deep gray followed by an ultimate darkness. Welcoming the illumination, my mind slipped into a much needed unconscious state.

Three

Beeping monitors echoed in my ears. The sound maximized the excruciating pound of my head as I slipped in and out of consciousness. Opening my eyes for what seemed like the thousandth time was still just as much a chore as it had been the first. I focused all my energy on the blinding light peering through my heavy lids. Trying to keep them open for even a few seconds was next to impossible. Darkness took over again, yet for the first time my mind stayed intact and continued to wander. I focused on my sense of touch.

I could feel a cool breeze coming in from the right. I wiggled my toes and lifted each of my fingers, yet the remainder of my body stayed motionless. How long had I been laying here, I wondered? I thought about my father and my cave. I allowed my body to relax and my mind to roam. Voices chimed in from what sounded like inches from my ears. Still unable to open my eyes or move my body toward them, I listened carefully.

"How's our boy?" I recognized Dr. Brooklyn's cheerful voice. I pictured her plump lips and magnetic eyes as I listened. The ache and crackling in my mind cleared as I focused to hear whomever she was talking to.

Another woman answered in a much less attractive tone. It was low and raspy.

"Hanging in there. He hasn't had any convulsions today, and his heart beat is no longer skipping or pausing. I think the serum finally took."

"Great! None of the surviving others are adjusting this quickly! If it's been a full day without troubling news, he should be as good as new before tomorrow. His healing powers should get stronger and stronger… if the serum is working properly, that is. Call me as soon as he's fully awake, Judy. I'm especially fond of this one."

"Yes ma'am." The raspy voice responded.

"Oh, and make sure to let our division controllers know he is waking up. I'm sure they're ready and waiting for his sound feed."

Especially fond!? I felt my heart beat faster in excitement. I could hear the beeping next to me increase in speed. The noises around me were intriguing, and at that very moment all I wanted to see was Dr. Brooklyn's gorgeous face. In a flash my eyes shot open. With my head remaining stuck in place, I searched the room for my doctor with my eyes only.

The brightness of the lights above me quickly faded, allowing all the other shapes in the room to take form. I could see every tiny detail, even the microscopic ones. A crack between the stucco on the ceiling, a glitch in the lines forming words on a mini monitor next to me, even the screws holding the door knob in place from across the room were clear and focused. But there were no people in sight.

Where was she? I wondered briefly if the injection had left me to hallucinate, that is until nurse Judy come waltzing into the room. I could hear a low humming of an unfamiliar tune escape from her throat. Her lips remained in place as she tried unsuccessfully to carry a nearly silent a tune in the back of her mouth. Her expression seemed caring and focused. The sound matched the voice I just listened to so intently. I realized instantly that although the conversation sounded like it took place within inches from my head, it had in fact been conducted in the hallway outside of my room. How could I hear a conversation so perfectly, when it was exchanged so far away?

I wanted desperately to shout out to her that I was awake, and that I wanted to see Dr. Brooklyn, nothing but a teeny squeak pushed through my lips. Nurse Judy didn't hear my miniature cry for help. She continued to stare at the brightly lit screen of a device she gripped in her wrinkled fingers. I watched her make her way to the other side of the room, and pick up a metal stick from on top of a long white counter top.

"Yes, I think he'll be waking up for good very soon." She said into the object.

I thought about a book of my fathers. One that I'd read countless times as a young boy. The book told of the characters frequently speaking to each other on a 'phone', whatever that was. As I laid there motionless, I wondered if this talking object the nurse was speaking into was in fact the same communication devise referred to in that book. My suspicions were later confirmed. Just as she set it down I faded back into unconsciousness.

Only a few hours passed when I jolted awake for a final time. Sitting straight up instantly, I began pulling the sticky objects from my skin in a panic. Energy, nothing but energy! My body tingled from the inside out as the energy exploding in my chest pulled me to my feet. What little color there was in this small white room, was sticking out like a sore thumb. Everything was vibrant and showing in much more detail than what I was used to.

I could hear the noises from outside my room, clear and in elaborated conversations. Voices flowed into my ears and fed the energy that was rapidly consuming me. No sooner than I had the stickies pulled off, nurse Judy rushed into the room and was at my side.

"Brooklyn!? Where is my doctor?" I shouted at her as I rushed from one side of the room to the other.

I shook my hands at my sides and ran awkwardly in place, trying to rid myself of the energy as it coursed through my veins.

"It's okay Jackson." She said calmly. Her voice was raspy yet comforting. "Concentrate my boy. Concentrate on your breathing and on my voice. Can you do that for me?"

Truly looking at Judy for the first time was hardly relaxing, yet her gaze did hold a motherly comfort. While trying to focus on her face as a whole, rather than each wrinkle and pore, I allowed myself to push some anxiety aside and speak, only moderately yelling.

"It burns and tingles. What is going on with my eyes!? I can hear everything!"

"Breath Jackson, just breath. Like I said, try to concentrate my boy."

She placed a comforting hand on my shoulder and raised her other arm into the air from her waist to her chest indicating deep breaths. I followed her lead. Though this did somewhat calm the nerves in my fingertips, it didn't even touch the energy advancing inside my core.

"You'll learn to control it, eventually. You'll get used to the tingle and the adrenaline, Jackson. But, until then, you'll need to try with all your might to focus... concentrate."

Her words were loud and overpowering as I continued to jog in place. My head shot back and forth searching the room for I don't know what. The confusion was engulfing. Too much noise. I couldn't focus only on the sound of Judy's voice, when more than a dozen others were intruding into my mind. I could hear EVERYTHING. I looked back at Judy as she repeated herself over and over.

"Focus, Jackson. Focus on only me."

I watched her mouth moving in unison with her words everything else slowly faded into the distance. The noise from outside the room was now a mere whisper. I concentrated on Judy, and Judy alone.

"That's it, Jack. You can do this. Only look at me, and only listen to me... concentrate."

Holding still was proving to be impossible. Though my mind was thinking only of Judy to drown out my surroundings, my body was still pulsing with a strange prickling. I felt like I could run for days without tiring. And that's all I wanted to do, run. I fought every ounce of it as every part of me wanted to take off into a sudden sprint.

"You got this Jack. Just keep your eyes on me. You can run in place all you want, just listen to my voice and keep your mind focused." Her coaching remained slow and steady. "Dr. Brooklyn is on her way now, Jackson. You're doing an amazing job. Just keep listening to my voice."

After a few more minutes of focusing on nurse Judy's coaching, Dr Brooklyn burst through the door. Behind her, hurried a young man pushing a folded-up machine, much like the one I had in my room. I'd used it every day in the previous weeks to run on. The boy looked to be in his mid-teens. He quickly unfolded the machine allowing half of it to fall to the floor. He pressed a few buttons all the while avoiding eye contact with Dr. Brooklyn and myself.

Taking as long to set up the machine as it took Dr. Brooklyn to rush across the room, he exited, just as hurried as he had entered. My curiosity for this young boy quickly faded as I met eyes with Dr. Brooklyn. My now enhanced vision only maximized her beauty. I was momentarily lost in her charm, pausing from my jitters for a fraction of a second before the energy surged back through me.

Dr. Brooklyn pointed at the machine, "Please." She urged, indicating for me to help myself onto it. She continued to speak as I leaped onto the machine and ran full speed ahead. "Wow Jackson! You seem to have even more energy than we anticipated. How do you feel?"

"Jack!" I shouted. "Just Jack!" The static in my ears was returning and the detail of my sight faded in and out as I quickened my pace. Faster and faster I ran, trying to force the overpowering energy out of my body. "I feel strange... very strange!" I yelled.

"I do recall the injected animals having a similar surge of energy as they came into consciousness. They jolted from one end of their cages to the other for some time. Eventually they were able to control it. They grew accustomed to their new bodies."

"How long is it going to take?" I demanded.

"I'm not sure, Jack. You're the first human injected to awake fully. You're much more advanced than any of the others. We're not quite sure what to expect out of you yet."

My body continued to push forward. I focused my sight on one spot on the wall, not allowing myself to get distracted by anything else in the room, especially Dr. Brooklyn's beauty. Looking straight forward allowed me to focus my ears on the doctor's voice, rather than getting caught up on the details of her face. I couldn't bear to let all the other noise around interfere with my thoughts. I had to have a conversation with Dr. Brooklyn... a real conversation without distractions.

I had to know what was going to happen with me, and I needed to find out about the other men and women who had been waiting in that uncomfortable white waiting room.

"I woke up before. I couldn't move, but I could hear you talking about the surviving others." Trying to lower my voice was proving to be a difficult task. "What did you mean by that?" I continued to shout. My legs still carrying me faster and faster as we spoke.

"We have only been able to find twelve of you total containing the G-Factor. You're the last to join our cause. Upon finding you, we split everyone into two groups. The healthiest, like yourself, were injected with the stronger more advanced dose. Only three of you survived." She hesitated and her voiced saddened, but she continued. I listened intently. "The other, weaker half of the group were injected with the lesser technology. A serum allowing The Company's eyes and ears into their bodily systems, but without any extras."

"Define extras!" I yelled, continuing my sprint.

"Extras as in the boost in your immune, circulatory, respiratory and nervous systems. You'll be stronger in every way Jack, as I told you before. Even your mental retention will increase. You'll retain more than 75% more knowledge than you were able to before. A photogenic mind so to speak. In simpler terms, you went from having a regular functioning brain and body to having an extraordinarily advanced brain and body."

She tried to continue but I cut her off. I could sense the excitement rising and I was in no mood for her uplifted spirits. Did she not care about the people who died in their stupid little experiment? Rather than holding in my anger and trying to keep my voice down I let this rapidly forming hatred for The Company out. The anger was surging through me along with the adrenaline. "How many of the weaker group died?" I demanded.

"Four, Jack. We lost more than half of them." Dr. Brooklyn replied quietly.

"Four!? You lost more than Half!! And if only three of us stronger group lived then that means YOU and this COMPANY murdered seven people, and for what?!?" I shouted. "So you can send us out like your little pets to do your dirty work?! I don't want to be here with you, sick people! I don't want to fight for you. I don't want to feel like this! I want to go home to my cave and my father!"

I continued to run faster and faster as I shouted. The bottoms of my feet burned, but I didn't care. The pain only fueled my adrenaline. I could feel my chest rise and fall rapidly, though not from tiring. I tried to think back to the waiting room and picture those who awaited their fate by my side. Not one particular face came to mind. Had I really been too afraid and self-absorbed to remember any of their faces?

"Jackson, I understand why you're upset. I also understand how different your body must feel right now." She sounded calm, confident, and compassionate. "Along with everything else enhanced inside you, your emotions will run stronger. You must learn to control that along with every other part of your body and senses. That's why these first couple weeks upon your awakening are so critical. If you are unable to control yourself, then I assure you The Company will not put up with it."

"I don't care about The Company, their hidden agendas, or about how they *handle* me Brooklyn! I just want to get the hell out of here!" I yelled as I continued to pick up the speed, holding back the tears as they formed behind my eyes.

The pounding of several heavy boots thudded up the hallway, clearly into my hearing range. I could tell they were headed in my direction, but I couldn't tell how far away they were. I recalled Dr. Brooklyn telling me that The Company would be able hear and see everything I could hear and see. As the running boots approached, I realized that nothing I said from here on out would be safe from their invasive ears... ever.

The metal phone setting on the counter top across the room rang. Judy picked it up with a quick and panicked.

"Hello?"

She silenced for only a few seconds while she listened. I focused on the voice coming through the other end. I managed to get a grip on my rising anger and in turn tried to lower my voice. I answered the old man's question before she had a chance to. Making my words slow, calm, and clear, I knew they could hear my answer without needing Judy to relay my response. I looked up from my focal point on the wall and gazed into the camera peering down at me from the corner of the room.

"No. Your approaching soldiers don't need to net me, shock me, or take me out! I'm not a threat, and I don't need to be gunned down or restrained."

Abruptly stopping from my sprint, I planted my feet firmly in place and glared into the screen of the camera. It took everything I had to hold my body stiff and strong. I thought about my father as he screeched my name. I thought about the burn of the injection as it was forced into my veins. Dr. Brooklyn's warnings of The Company bounced around my angry mind.

I'll do as they say in self-preservation, I thought. Unable to speak my true intentions aloud. I made a silent vow to myself at that very moment that The Company would pay for what they were doing to me. And they'd pay for all the others who died in this whole injection process. I'd fight. And I'd do as they tell me to, but only until the moment was right. I'd learn to defeat the serpent and whatever else they put in front of me. But, when it came down to my true intentions, I'd find whoever was in charge within The Company walls. Even if it took years to make the final move, I'd avenge all those whom The Company had killed or harmed. From that moment forward I'd keep my most important thoughts to myself. I'd harness the anger inside me until the perfect time. By creating this serum, The Company had unknowingly created their own enemy.

Judy and Dr. Brooklyn gasped and stared at me. I could feel their eyes peering in my direction as their shocked faces twisted in my reaction to the phone call. The men running down the hallway abruptly stopped outside the door. I could hear their winded breaths as I stood with my own lungs thriving in steady breath. I held my confident gaze at the camera and steadied the shake in my hands. The unfathomable notion to hold still nearly consumed me, as the energy threatened to push my entire body into convulsions. I held strong, not allowing the inner force and emotions to surface. Without trouble, I heard the deep voice on the other end of the phone, that was still pressed securely against my nurse's ear.

"Judy, the men are there and on standby if needed."

Again, I spoke in her place, "I assure you sir, they won't be."

I looked back over at Dr. Brooklyn's surprised yet seemingly proud expression. After listening to the click of the phone as the man hung up his end I spoked candidly to them both.

"I can do this Dr., but you have to be patient with me and I'll need a lot of help." After swallowing my pride and containing the energy that was still coursing throughout me, I sat down on the edge of the bed. "Where do we start?" I asked.

Dr. Brooklyn's smile widened, and her eyes displayed a twinkle as she looked me up and down.

"I can see that your physique is already improving, Jack. But, before we can begin your recovery we must first remove the remainder of your... um..." She coughed a little into a balled fist, and searched for a word I'd recognize. "Your remaining tubes."

"What do you mean? I pulled everything off!"

Dr. Brooklyn pointed towards my belt line, and then lifted a quizzical brow.

"I'll leave you with nurse Judy now. She'll be your right hand for the weeks to come. She'll be here for your every need, it will do you good to comply with her, Jack. Be kind, for the two of you will get to know each other well. As soon as she has you taken care of here, she'll escort you to your new apartment. At that point you'll eat and begin the relax and knowledge phase. I'll meet up with you there."

She turned swiftly on one heal and exited the room. I glanced up at my nurse confused, to see her smiling warmly... motherly.

Taking stalk of my exposed arms and chest left me more than a little impressed. Though not much bigger in diameter, I was very much more cut and defined. My arms, shoulders, and abs were also more toned, and my pigment seemed darker and healthier in color.

I thought for sure I'd detached everything from my body when I jolted awake. I tugged at the waist line of my gray sweatpants a little embarrassed, yet very painstakingly curious. With ever widening eyes I nearly passed out at the sight of the tube extending from my member. It led to a plastic bag secured to my thigh. "What the hell is this?" I squeaked.

Nurse Judy giggled at my reaction. "It's called a catheter, Jack. It's to catch your urine. Now let's slip off those skivvies and get rid of it. It appears you're fully functional and will no longer be needing it."

Completely mortified I rolled back, gripped the edges of the bed and prepared myself for the painful violation to begin.

Four

Once all the tubes were removed and a few blood tests were ran, Judy led me back to my in-house apartment. Following her through the halls was much different than it had been when I was led by David. She walked quicker, knowing how badly I needed to constantly move my body. My hands shook at my sides and tapped the outer edges of my legs as we rounded one corner after another toward my room.

The structure of The Company would take some getting used to. It was like a maze engulfing me, making me feel smaller with each step. I was growing to hate the confinement. I longed to feel the earths cool soft mud between my toes, and the fresh crisp air in my lungs.

There were much less passersby in the hallway now than there had been in the journey out of my room. We only passed two people. It was a young couple, holding hands and grinning as they came into view. I could hear them coming long before I could see them round the corner. They stopped dead in their tracks at the sight of me. The woman whispered into her companion's ear. I could hear her words loud and clear. Their distance made no difference, I heard her as if the soft whispers were in my own ear, and as close to me as she was to him.

"Is that him?" She asked. "Do you think that's Jackson?"

"I don't know, Love." He gently replied. "But we best not stare."

The young lover nodded her head in agreement and they again continued to walk in our direction. He was able to keep his eyes from mischievously glancing in my direction, she was not. I suppose curiosity was stronger than her intent on maintaining good manners. Her eyes locked onto mine as they came closer.

"To answer your question, Ma'am, yes I am Jackson."

I informed the girl as they reached my side.

Gasps escaped their lips as they stopped a mere two feet away from me and stared. The color in the girls face quickly changed in pigment to a shade of light pink. She flushed and giggled unable to say anything more. I smiled at her warmly. I'd never made a girl blush before, and to be honest I quite liked it.

I ran my jittery hands, that were still just as full of electricity, through my hair. It was thick, much thicker than the last time I'd felt it, and shorter. Upon feeling the top of my head, I let my hand slide down the sides of my face and scratch the bottom of my chin. My beard was trimmed to stubble. I noticed the girl drop the man's hand and hold her breath as she watched my fingers move through my healthy mane. She was wide eyed and with her mouth slightly ajar. The boy scowled at me hard, before clasping his fingers back around hers.

"Come on, Claira, we have to go!" He snorted.

Not allowing me to watch them walk way, nurse Judy chuckled and continued her stride.

"Come along, Jackson, we've got to get you nourished and we have a lot of work to do."

I agreed with a nod, jumped up and down in place on a few times, and shook my arms to my sides, then followed directly behind her. The couple didn't speak another word to each other. Judy talked over her shoulder towards me as she pushed through a set of double doors. Soon, we entered the last hallway.

"You do know that you shouldn't flirt with every girl that looks in your direction, right?"

"What do you mean?" I wondered.

"Especially the ones who are already spoken for."

Judy stopped at the door to my room which contained the same lime green numbers that were above the others leading to Dr. Brooklyn's office and the lab. I looked up at the color and then down the hall at each of the other doors. Only two others contained this color. For the first time since I'd awoke, the intruding hum of other conversations coming from the rooms we were passing had stilled. It was finally somewhat quiet. An awkward silence swirled around my anxious mind. Judy stood in front of me with a look of amusement. She must have been taking in my curiosity.

"Did you hear what I said, Jackson?" she asked. "Or are you too busy looking pointlessly down an empty hallway to hear my words?"

"Yes, Ma'am I heard you. But, what do you mean exactly?"

"Well to be honest, Jack, they couldn't have found a more handsome young man to inject. And now with your flawless skin, enhanced features and muscle mass. I can only imagine the attention you're going to get." Her look was serious and compassionate. "Just be careful, Jack. Stay focused and don't let yourself get distracted by women. Especially ones who have been born and raised within The Company walls. They're vultures. Believe me I know. Self-centered spoiled rotten brats, every last one of them. Landing you will surely be a sport to them, if nothing else. Do you get that?"

"Yes, Ma'am." I replied, though I wasn't quite sure what to make out of her advice. What did she mean by sport, or landing? This new world would take some getting used to. All the women in my village were either older or younger than I by at least ten years. Seeing a pretty face close to my age hadn't just been a rarity, it was nonexistent. Not letting myself become distracted by women would be next to impossible. I wondered if that's why I had such a strong pull toward my doctor. I quickly dismissed the thought and pushed Dr. Brooklyn's face to the back of my mind.

Judy pointed at a little plastic box that was attached to the wall next to my door. She informed me to waive my wrist in front of the box. Upon following instructions there was a small beeping noise and my door clicked open. She explained to me that inside my wrist was a chip. The chip was my personal identification key. A key that would grant me access into any door I was authorized to enter, whether it be within this building or any other belonging to The Company.

How could this be, I wondered? I twisted my wrist in circles, wriggled my fingers, and then held my arm up to the light to inspect it. I could see nothing under the skin, it made no sense. Judy chuckled at my naive curiosity before nudging me with her shoulder to go inside. I shook my head and bunched my face to one side. What else was implanted and technologically altered inside my body? Was there room for more? Was I even human anymore? A part of me grew in anger, and another part of me felt an unwelcomed sense of shame... teetering the edge of embarrassment.

Once inside, a heavenly scent consumed my nostrils. Prepared and ready to devour was an outrageous display of fresh fruits and steamed vegetables, along with poached salmon and some fluffy bread. It was melt in your mouth perfection. This room was much different than my last one. Yet, it was still quite easy for me to take in every detail.

My eyes scanned the space from one end to the other. I picked up on every shade of every color. An imprint of the place seared permanently in mind, the entire place would forever stick in detailed memory. Rather than the place I had before, with one giant open space containing my eating space, a bed, and running machine. I now had an extremely welcoming living condition. My bedroom and bathroom were in separate, more private, spaces than the dining, living, and workout area.

As I relished my meal, Judy explained to me how the nicest apartments within The Company were reserved for only the most important personnel. I was now considered to be amongst them. We were in the West, Third Division Wing. A place I'd learn to love, appreciate, and despise all at once. A place of retreat to call my own, but it would never really be home. Rather than mincing words, I cut right to the chase with Judy. I made a quick a mental note as not to give away Johnson nor his intentions, I'd need to choose my words carefully.

"Dr. Brooklyn said that injecting us was no longer an experiment but a necessity. What did she mean by that?" I asked.

Judy's face petrified, her eyes grew cold, and her lips pursed. She finished chomping the bite of food in her mouth and swallowed with a strained gulp.

"There's a monster out there, Jack. The Company needs your help in fighting it."

"Lamians?" I asked.

"Yes! How do you know this?" She demanded. Judy looked nervously back and forth around the room, as if to make sure no one was lurking around the corners.

"No one is here, Ma'am. I would've heard, or even smelled them I'm sure." I rolled my eyes a half circle, only starting the notion before I stopped myself. Did she not realize that there was no need to spy on me, when I myself was now their spy? I pointed to my head and lifted my eyebrows as if to hint to her what was going on. She caught onto my indirect notion instantly, and let her held breath out, she surrendered.

"Oh yes, yes! I guess it's going to take some getting used to for all of us, Jack. Not just yourself." She sighed. "So, tell me then. How do you know about the Lamians?"

"I heard some crazy story about an ancient serpent called Lamia, from a drifter some time back. I don't remember much details about him or his name."

I lied. "I just remember the name of the beasts, and that they're half human half snake. Can you tell me more about them?"

"No!" She shouted, and then paused to gather herself from the outburst. "I mean yes, there are serpents out there that you'll be meant to fight, and they are in fact called Lamians, but this is nor the time or place to be discussing it. We're all under strict instructions not to do so. When the time is right you'll meet the lead man in the military department. He'll tell you all you need to know at that time." Judy looked down at her half empty plate and continued to shovel more food into her mouth. "Right now, we have to focus on you and how we're going to get you to control your body. Once we have that down, you'll learn and train. Not until all of this is accomplished will you meet the military department and learn of the Lamians."

"I think I'm doing pretty good at control." I stated proudly, as I scooped in another bite of broccoli.

"HA!" It wasn't a real laugh, so much as a mocking grunt. "You haven't held your body still for more than five seconds since you woke up Jackson Bellony. You're even making me anxious and that's rare! There is much work to be done!"

She motioned with her hand for me to look across the table.

I glanced back and forth at the food and dishes that were bouncing and clanking across the table top. It took me a second to realize that my knee hitting the bottom of the table was the culprit of the traveling food. I tried unsuccessfully to stop bouncing my heel on the floor. Upon holding my leg still, the jitters moved involuntarily through the rest of my body, leaving me to wiggle and shift in my chair. I clanked my spoon against the table's edge between bites.

Judy remained calm and nurturing.

"It's okay, Jack. As soon as we're done eating you can run, and we'll get started early on the knowledge phase. They wanted us to wait a couple of days for that, but I think The Company will agree with me that you're ready."

She smiled kindheartedly, and we enjoyed the rest of our meal in silence.

As soon as our bellies were full, Judy gave me a quick tour of my new accommodations. First explaining the bathroom in a bit fuller detail than the computerized voice had before. This left me a tad bit embarrassed. I wondered why The Company had allowed me to relieve myself on and next to the plant in the corner of the room, rather than the "toilet", as Judy called it. It even grossed me out a little to think that I'd used the water out of the bowl to wash myself.

Though I figured Judy had been informed of my previously barbaric toiletry habits, she never mentioned it. I'd read of apartments and bathrooms and showers in my father's books. At the time, it was all just gibberish to me, meaningless words. Anything I'd read that I was unable to picture, or understand, I blocked out while reading. At the time, it had been as if the letters before my eyes had formed nothing but blank pages and an empty imagination. Though I recalled reading words like sink, tap, bathtub, and toilet paper, I was oblivious and equally careless to their meanings.

Judy left me to a moment on my own and informed me to take my time washing up. Taking my time is exactly what I did. I got my first REAL shower. Wow, was that amazing!? It was like standing under a powerfully heated waterfall. Temporarily, it calmed my anxious nerves, relaxed my muscles, and slowed my jitters. I learned quickly that showers were heaven.

I wrapped myself in one of the large fluffy towels that were hanging on the wall by the shower. I was left feeling refreshed, and for a moment I was somewhat comforted. I was starting to get used to the power surge pulsing through my body. In a way, I was even starting to like it. It reminded me of the way my body felt after chasing down a kill in the woods by my cave. The anxiety of it all was melting away, leaving only adrenaline and excitement. It was making me feel ambitious and charged. Not only like I could accomplish anything in the world, but like I could do it in record time. I felt invincible, powerful even. I'd only been awake for a few short hours and my body was adapting like a pro.

I stared into a giant mirror that hung across the length of an entire wall. I was amazed. I stood in awe. It may have been the longest I held my body still yet, while I took stalk of the man in front of me. He looked much like the old me, only better. I couldn't believe what I was seeing. I flexed the muscles in my arms first, then my chest and legs, checking out every angle.

I'd become a whole new man, basically overnight. I'd seen my own refection from bits and pieces of glass before, but never in full length. There was a woman in my village who went to the market place every few months to trade pieces of an old broken mirror from before the lightning storm. She must've had a pretty large supply stashed away somewhere, because she never seemed to run out. My father and I acquired a few pieces from her over the years.

The shape of my face remained the same, with a prominent jaw and strong cheek bones. Yet, my skin was no longer damaged from the long years living out in the dirt and dry wind. I didn't need to look closely because I could already see in such detail. My pores were now practically nonexistent. Like porcelain, there wasn't a wrinkle or scar. Heat was radiating off my body and every inch of me was solid as stone.

I shook my head in disbelief, before giving myself a quick wink and handsome smile. I'm sure The Company loved that. I was feeding them exactly what they wanted. I recalled my father telling me at a very young age to keep your friends close and your enemies closer. I hadn't had a clue on what he meant by that at the time. As I stood naked in a strange place observing myself as a restructured man, I knew exactly what he was talking about.

I dressed quickly and then exited the bathroom, refreshed and ready to start whatever learning process The Company had prepared for me. I thought about my father too much. I missed him and needed his advice now more than ever. So, I did the best I could do, and that's everything I imagined he'd want me to. Nothing more and nothing less.

More than anything, I wanted to portray myself as the man he taught me to be. I'd make the best of the anything and everything thrown in my direction. I'd think tactically, just as he taught me to. We were survivors, my father and me. Whether he was at my side to see it or not, I wanted to make him proud.

My relaxing calm and quiet environment didn't last long. I ran for some time on the familiar machine that Judy finally explained to be a treadmill. The same sticky devises were placed onto my head and chest, just as before. As I ran Judy explained the schedule we were to follow over the next few days. I pushed my body to its maximum speed and it was exhilarating. It helped me to focus my mind on conversation, rather than my exceeding energy.

Judy let her fingers go to work on the strange hand-held devise she'd clutched since I first awoke. She explained to me that with this devise she was able to log and keep track of my progress, as well as control every characteristic of the apartment. As she was explaining, a very large yet skinny box rose from the floor in front of me.

"This is a television, Jack. You'll watch it while you run. With your brain retention you should be a quick study. All you need to do is keep your eyes on the screen and pay attention."

She pressed a few more buttons on the hand held, or "tablet" as she called it, and then made herself comfortable on a sofa across the room.

Words and figures danced across the screen in front of me, it was magical. I listened to the voice coming out of the television explain the details and history of The Company and of the creation and technology of the harnessed power source. I was memorized, and absorbed every word like a sponge. I'm not exactly sure how long I listened and watched before the voices on the screen were very rudely interrupted by the sound of screaming coming from outside the apartment. I stopped my jog and shouted at Judy.

"Turn it off!" I jumped off the treadmill and stared at her, eyes wide. "Don't you hear that?" I naively demanded.

Judy jumped to her feet and pressed a button on her devise. Everything in the room seemed to freeze including her and the television. Her face was blank, of course Judy couldn't hear anything, what was I thinking? She watched me with her eyes just as wide as mine, not moving a morsel as she strained to hear anything at all.

"Someone is hurt!" I ran to the door and started waiving my wrist back and forth in the air. "Why isn't it opening?!"

"Jack, you only need to use your key to enter places, not to exit. All you have to do is twist the handle." As I reached for the handle she grabbed my hand sternly. "Stop, Jack!" She snatched my attention and I stared into her eyes. The screeching outside the apartment was still approaching, but I focused everything I could on Judy. "This is what we talked about in controlling your emotions. You need to learn to calm yourself and assess situations, Jack. You can't just react, you need to think. If you go out this door, be very cautious, please! Don't make any rash decisions!"

I knew Judy was right the instant she spoke. This didn't make it any easier for me. The screeching voice sounded like it was in much pain. I swung the door open, nearly ripping it off the hinges. Judy failed miserably at keeping up. She yelled in my direction.

"Jackson! Think about what you're doing!"

Five

I'll never forget the first time I saw Amber. As her screaming stilled, the soft chirping of small plastic wheels screeched in my eardrums. Four men, one on each corner of a hospital bed, escorted the now shocked into submission girl who was strapped onto it. None of them looked in my direction. Their faces were flat, as if this was a normal situation.

I stopped in my tracks from a dead run to observe her. They sped walked passed me through the hall, rushed and with a purpose. They were followed by David and another man in a matching white coat with a green undershirt. Neither of them showed a hint of concern. I refused to glance up and absorb the detail at any of the men, as I was captivated with the unconscious girl. Her long, dirty blonde hair nearly drug the floor as it hung off the moving bed. A drip of saliva escaped from the corner of her perfectly defined and nearly red in pigment lips. Her neck and shoulder twitched, along with her knees and ankles. The whites of her eyes were all I could see, as the color was rolled back inside of her head.

"David!" I shouted, and followed at his side. "Who is this? What's wrong with her?"

"Jackson, meet Amber." He spoke with flat sarcasm. "She too was injected, but apparently didn't wake up as pleasant as yourself."

David stopped to look at me, leaving the other men pushing her in their continued rush. His eyes traveled down, and then back up the length of my body with a puzzled furrow in his brow.

"Why aren't you in your room, Jackson?" He glared at Judy who was just now reaching our side, huffing and puffing, and crouched over to grab her knees. She stood straight, took in a breath, and opened her mouth to explain. I interrupted.

"I heard the screaming, so I had to see!" I defended.

David glared for some time back and forth at the two of us, but not before rolling his eyes and shaking his head in disgust. He leaned forward and up onto his toes. He looked deep into my eyes. I could tell that he wasn't looking at me, so much as through me.

"So, we have a caveman superhero, and a melodramatic, panic attacking Company princess."

David shook his head again and then turned on his heels to strut away. There was no need to say much more. Judy and I both knew that he was speaking directly to The Company men and women peering through my eyes. He had a good point, although it was still an arrow's shot to the heart for me. What did he think, I wanted to be there? I was growing to dislike David more by the second.

"Don't worry about him, Jackson. He's just mad that he stopped growing before his teen years." Judy joked and placed a welcomed hand on my shoulder. "Let's just get back to the room, okay? We should be expecting Dr. Brooklyn any time now, and there is still much to be learned."

After agreeing with Judy, I reluctantly held her same pace as we marched back to my living quarters. I didn't feel much like talking after seeing Amber's drooling face and convulsing body. So many questions were still swarming around in my head, but I didn't care much to ask. Amber's apartment was one door down from mine, allowing me to hear the conversations of her nurse, David and the other men assisted her in restraint and confinement.

Amber's nurse must've been the other man in the white coat and green undershirt, I concluded. I asked Judy if I could run in the quiet of the room for a while without the television or anything else clouding my mind. I asked her kindly if I could be alone with my thoughts for a while, to work everything out in mind. I didn't want her to know that too much noise would enable me from listening into the apartment room next to my own.

Judy complied, and I listened… very intently to the conversation an apartment away. Clearly, David didn't have much faith in the whole operation. One of the men, on the other hand, seemed much more optimistic. The conversation was mostly held between the two of them. An occasional yes, no, or disappointed grunt would periodically escape from the other two.

Amber woke with a bone chilling screech more than once, but she was quickly silenced. I wondered what they must've been doing to her to keep her still, and I wondered why The Company would allow it. That is until I put the pieces together myself. They were using her to listen in on David and the nurse. I recalled lying awake and overhearing Dr. Brooklyn's conversation. The Company must've been doing the same through the ears of Amber.

Though angered at first by the thought, I realized that by staying in my room and doing nothing to stop the inhumanity, merely so that I could listen in and spy myself, I was displaying the exact same behavior. I wasn't quite sure how to feel about the epiphany. The guilty fact made me sick to my stomach, yet I continued the insanity, unable to resist the unnecessary gossip. They spoke of the injection and about those who had passed away in the process. I ran faster on the treadmill as the anger filled me. It wasn't until they mentioned the serpent, that I slowed my pace and strained a little to overhear every single word.

"Do you think they'll be able to kill them?" The nurse bluntly asked.

"No, not really." David replied. "Haven't you seen the clips of them? I wouldn't count on anything being able to kill them. Especially since they only move at night, during the storm. Don't you ever wonder how they're able to slither away untouched when we bomb them?"

"Yeah I do!" Said the Nurse in excitement, almost as if they were exchanging the details of a scary made-up story to frighten a child. It was irritating to say the least. "My brother thinks God sent them to finish us off. You know, since we figured out how to live beyond the storm. He thinks the human race was meant to be killed off years ago, and that the Lamians are here to finish the job."

"What do you think?" David asked him.

"I don't know what to think, really. I just hope we can figure out their weak spot. I heard they're going to train these guys with sticks and swords." He laughed. "Like, if firepower can't penetrate them, then maybe a blade can."

"You think it's funny?" David snapped.

"Well, kind off…" the nurse paused. "It's like bringing a knife to a gun fight. What makes them think it'll do any good?"

David's tone relaxed as he sighed in surrender. "No good, I guess. I just hope this isn't all a giant waste of time. My wife is expecting… It's given me a different perspective on the future of mankind, and of The Company for that matter. If these surviving injected subjects can't help us, then I don't know what we'll do."

"Oh… well… congratulations." Stammered the nurse. I could feel the tension between them, as it were seeping through the walls of our apartments. Silence inevitably followed, only to be interrupted once again by the screeching Amber.

This was the fourth time she let out a painful scream since they reached her room. The quick paced tick of an awkward static cut off the wrenching noise of her squeal. I couldn't take it any longer.

"Judy?"

"Yes Jack."

"Can you hear her screaming at all?" I asked.

"Nope, I can't hear anything."

"They won't let her wake up." I informed her, concerned. "Every time she screams they're shutting her up with some sort of static. What do you think they're doing to her?"

"Shocking her most likely." Judy was clearly disgusted.

"Shock?" I hadn't a clue what she meant by that.

"Stay here, Jack. I'll be right back okay?"

"Are you going to help her?"

"Just stay here!" she shouted as the door slammed behind her on the way out.

I tried to hold still, while I concentrated on one thing. The focus was getting easier and easier. *I'll conquer this burning adrenaline yet*, I thought. Into my bedroom and directly to the wall that separated me from Amber, I hurried. With my ear pressed firmly against the wall as, I listened. Judy barged into the apartment demanding answers. She yelled at them, calling them names and words I hadn't yet been exposed to. I liked Judy.

Only a motherly figure could silence a room of grown men with words of disappointment and accused stupidity. She pointed out to them the fact that too much electrical shock could damage the altered cells. Amber's body was in a sensitive state, and these men were possibly ruining her future capabilities. And for what? So they could prolong the inevitable care they'd eventually have to render her.

I was more than impressed with Judy's spunk and character. I listened in as she instructed the men to wait in another room, out of sight while only her and nurse Brock were alone at Amber's side. She reminded Brock that he'd need to be a trusted shoulder for Amber to lean on. Someone she could turn to and rely on for help or answers. Allowing her to be hurt upon awakening was not a great start on their journey together.

I listened. Completely engrossed, I closed my eyes and focused on all the sounds. The hands of a ticking clock on the wall in her room. The bubbling of boiling water in her kitchen. Everything else was silent aside from the sound of

45

my own heartbeat drumming away at a rapid pace. Even the breaths of Judy and Brock carried across her room, through the wall, and into my own ears. After a few short minutes of anticipation, the noise of rubbing fabric chimed in.

The thrashing of Amber's body back and forth on the transported bed came first. I continued to listen as she muffled her screams and held back the notion to screech out in fear and pain, like she had before.

"Let me go!" The words finally formed, loud and painful.

I pulled my head away from the wall, no longer needing to listen closely to the silence. I could hear her plain as day. My stomach sunk for her. Thinking of the panic and energy as I awoke, I wondered how it would be to feel that while being strapped down and unable to move.

I took a few steps back and slowly sat on the corner of my fluffy bed. I'd have traded it all in for my tiny wooden cot, in my simple dugout cave with my father in a heartbeat. The days past had been ill-fitting and completely overwhelming. I leaned to the side, letting my body fall over onto the overly fluffed comforter. With my knees pulled into my chest, and my shoulders rocking, I listened to the pain in Amber's voice through the wall.

The ripping of her restraints tore through the air as Judy and Brock set her free. I imagined her pacing back and forth and running in place, as I had. Judy's words of comfort sounded in. What is this place, I wondered? So cold, and heartless. It seemed to be every man for himself in a scramble of impersonality. I closed my eyes and felt the strange new static pulse through me. Like the ripples in water left behind by a jumping fish, I felt the blood in my veins move. Shaking in fear, I listened to the entire scene play out in Amber's room.

It took some time for Brock and Judy to somewhat calm her. I remained in the fetal position and my body began to sweat as loneliness took a hold of me, yet again. Again, I tried to picture my father, clinging to the comfort his face's image brought me. I remembered the sky-blue in his eyes. He had a prominent scar on his left cheekbone. Some folks found it a distraction, but I hardly noticed it. As I shook in my bed the scar stood out in memory above any other feature.

It's strange, the little things you miss. I squeezed my eyes shut as tight as my lids would allow, and I tried to hear the sound of his voice. His patience and instruction raced throughout my memory as I recalled him sitting at arm's length next to me. He'd listen to me reading the book collection that my grandfather had acquired in his many travels. The deep scratch in his throat when he'd clear it before each conversation rang in my ears.

I thought back to as young as I could remember. Strong and determined were my father's hands, and steady was his stride. He was an admirable man. If it'd been he in my same situation he wouldn't be curled up in a ball on the bed in a weak and helpless state. I longed to feel the confidence and security he always presented himself with. No matter how hard I tried to reach into my inner self and pull out any resemblance of my father, I was unable. I covered my ears tightly with the palms of my hands, and I tried to drown out the sound of Amber yelling.

"Be strong!" I scolded myself aloud.

Just as my words escaped, Amber stilled.

"Who was that?" She shouted from the other room. "Who is yelling at me? Where did that come from?" Her demands were clearly aimed at me.

I perked up from my helpless position on the bed. Of course, she could hear me, I realized. Why did I not think of this before? Maybe having to focus on something she couldn't see in such overwhelming detail would help her.

"My name is Jackson Bellony."

I responded in the same average pitch that I would have spoken to anyone sitting directly at my side. All noise on the other side of the wall remained still. Amber was clearly trying to focus on me rather than on Judy or Brock. So, I continued.

"It gets better, I promise. You just have to calm down and breathe and focus."

"I can't!" she yelled. I recalled the same feeling, and inability to lower my voice.

"Ask them for your treadmill." I instructed. "Running will help, and don't look at anyone. Keep your eyes straight ahead. Find a blank spot on the wall and listen to my voice."

I paced back and forth at the foot of my bed. A small tapping from Amber's floor rang in while she yelled for a treadmill. I could only guess it to be the sound of her feet hitting the ground while she jogged and jumped around, just like as I had. Judy excused herself, as well as David and the other men who were on standby, although they didn't go far.

I could hear their footsteps stop in the hallway between Amber's room and my own. They mumbled amongst each other about me. I didn't care much about what they had to say. I was much more concerned with Amber and her well-being. She was feeling the same way I was only a short time before, and I was determined to help her. As soon as I heard the sound of the moving treadmill, I turned away from the gossip in the hallway and spoke to Amber.

"Better?" I asked.

"Not really!" She shouted. "Who the hell are you, Jackson? Why am I hearing voices?"

"I'm not just a voice. I'm in the apartment room next to yours. I was injected too. Apparently, we can hear very well. Please call me Jack."

Amber and I soon held a steady conversation. I coached her for some time, giving her tips on calming her nerves. Eventually the nurse's aides outside of our apartments moved on to other things, and Judy made herself comfortable in the kitchen, granting me privacy with Amber. A trusting bond had already formed with Judy. I was grateful to have her around, as was Amber. Brock on the other hand, was not yet as welcomed. Amber had looked up to him in a plea for help too many times before enduring excruciating shocks as a result.

Dr. Brooklyn came to Amber's room before my own, only to be screamed at and ultimately dismissed. She made her way into my living quarters next. I excused myself from Amber, informing her to eat the food prepared. We'd pick up where we left off soon, and in the mean time I'd entertain conversation with our doctor. I knew that Amber would be listening in on me, all the same as I would her. She reluctantly agreed, all the while yelling at Brock.

"Well then… where is my food?" She demanded.

Amber was born and raised within The Company walls. She'd never experienced the outer world. She was full of spit-fire attitude, yet she knew nothing of the outdoors. I was the exact opposite of Amber in every way. We had much to learn from one another. Our short conversation consisted mainly of details about the injection. I informed her of how many died and that there was one more survivor. We could only hope that he'd be within hearing range soon. We had so much to discuss, it was no wonder Amber was reluctant to veer her attention from myself.

I stopped at my bedroom door, pausing at the handle in wait. Dr. Brooklyn wasn't alone with Judy. There was someone else close by, I could smell him. There was a powerful scent of sweat, smothered by a foreign musk. Introductions were made, and I listened as Judy welcomed our guest. I found it interesting that they'd allow a man that my own nurse had never even met into our living quarters on the same day as I awoke from the injection.

Six

Major Kenley J. Kingston stood with a strong posture and an even stronger presence. Confidence radiated from this man. He took my palm into his, squeezed it tightly, and gave it a slow. determining shake.

"Nice, strong handshake Jackson. Looks like your doctor wasn't exaggerating about your unexpectedly fast adaptation to the serum. That is good news."

I folded my arms across my chest in the same manner I had several times in the marketplace. I really missed standing side by side with my father in this exact same position, anytime a trade was to be sized up and carried out. I assumed the familiar stance and sized up the officer who stood in front of me. His t-shirt was tight, showing off the curves of each muscle protruding from his chest and arms. His face was serious, although I did have a hard time getting past his eyebrows. They were long, shaggy, and peppered thickly with aged gray. The brows were out of place on an otherwise slicked-bald head.

I shook off the notion to stare. I knew full well that they were my guests, rather than the other way around. I offered the doctor and officer a seat. Although I'd only just been introduced to my new living conditions, they were still mine. My father taught me to be a hospitable man no matter how sketchy the guests may be. He also taught me to be on guard, alongside the hospitality. He taught me to be ready for anything, yet never lose sight of myself and what I stood for.

"If you don't mind, Jackson, I think I'll stand." The Major said.

"Not at all Sir, and please, its Jack."

"Alright then, Jack it is. and you may call me Major Kingston."

There was no need for further small talk or meaningless chatter. Major Kingston cut right to the chase. He was a busy man, or so he claimed. He had much work to do and was running out of precious time. I stood my firm, making a mental note not to shift or shuffle my feet. I could sense the importance of focus and concentration, along with my capability of controlling my body.

Major Kingston seemed like a man of little patience when it came to childlike behavior. I could only assume that the inability to maintain self-control would be considered by him as such. I locked down the anxiety and adrenaline deep within my chest, and I planted my feet. After pressing a few buttons on her tablet, Judy sat back on the couch and watched the television rise. We locked eyes briefly before she flashed me a pitiful grin, and she flinched her head to the screen.

"Jack, the process of recovery we had planned for you has very recently been altered. As I'm sure you were informed we had intended on giving you, along with the others like you, a couple of weeks to rest, study, and adapt. I'm sorry to tell you that a couple of weeks is no longer a luxury any of us will be privilege to. I am about to show you something that will come off as very violent and disturbing. Before I press play I need to know that you can handle yourself and your emotions. I am counting on you Jack. I will explain what is going on as the video plays. In narration so to speak. Can I count on you to maintain self-control and hold any questions until I'm finished?"

"Yes, Sir." I hesitated but made the commitment.

The giant screen in front of me came to life. Running back and forth in the sand were several children. Not many trees were in sight, only rolling hills of sand and clay huts.

"This is a small village, less than one hundred miles away from where we are now. The Company has planted several cameras across the land in all directions. They're monitoring human life outside our safe zone. This is one of the largest known villages that hasn't been destroyed by the lightning. Yet, what you're watching now took place just yesterday afternoon."

The Major held a professional tone as he explained. I admired, and I envied the children on the screen. A ball was tossed back and forth amongst them. They ran freely, laughing and enjoying their lives without a care in the world.

"Nurse, will you fast forward until the sun fades and the sky darkens, please?"

The orders were followed. A blur of light and speed flashed before my eyes. I maintained my confident stance with arms folded and feet unmoving. I stole a quick glance at Judy, the beautiful yet strangely silenced Dr. Brooklyn, and

Major Kingston. It was od, but unmistakably, I could see a hint of sadness in their eyes.

I listened in on Amber and her nurse briefly while I awaited Major Kingston's instructions for Judy to continue the tape. They were still enjoying their meal. Amber was brushing off Brock's words, still in refusal to speak with him. She was listening in on us, too, no doubt. I could tell already that Amber was smarter and much more capable than she'd been given credit for. Perhaps it was the fact that I could now relate to her, or maybe even the simplicity of our easily carried conversation.

Whatever the reasoning, I was drawn to her. More so than to Dr. Brooklyn, who happened to be within arm's reach. Mesmerized by the recording on the television, and mentally distracted by Amber in the apartment next door, I could now care less about my doctor. She was merely a pretty face and nothing more.

Upon instruction, Judy continued to play the recording. Darkness consumed the screen, lit up only by periodic flashes of light from the sky. One flash after another, the village huts would appear out of the darkness only to be re-consumed within seconds.

"This took place last night, just after sundown. The lightning had only just begun." As the next flash of light lit up the screen, a figure appeared. "Pause it!" He jumped. The screen froze, and in front of me was a gruesome heart wrenching scene. The women in the room gasped. I held my breath, and I swallowed the lump in my throat. The Major remained emotionless.

The creature's eyes glowed in the reflection of the light. Long, black hair hung down her nude body, covering her breasts, reaching down past her stomach, and ending at a line of black and silver shimmering scales. In the clutches of her deadly grasp was the body of a limp man.

"This, Jackson, is the largest Lamian we've caught on video yet, and she's headed straight in our direction."

Eyre and lingering, the word *Lamian* echoed in my head. She wasn't at all what I'd pictured from Johnson's tale. This was much worse. The human portion of her body was nearly three times the size of the dead man's that she held in her arms. The snake portion wrapped around itself and intertwined between the homes of the innocent families. They were about to be slaughtered right before my eyes. There was no way to tell just how far her length could reach. What stood out more than anything else, were her blood-stained fangs. The long, sharp, venomous fangs were bearing. With a mouth stretched open at an impossible width, and evil in her gaze, her extended dripping fangs were hanging down just above the stomach of the dead man.

"Now Judy, after you press play I want you to re-pause the recording with each lightning flash. This will allow us to see how fast she moves, and the destruction she is capable of."

I masked my fear with an unreadable face and motionless body. Each time the video paused, the creature had another person or sometimes even two at a time, within her grasp. She moved from one side of the television screen to the other at an alarming speed, leaving the bodies of the dead piled up on the ground beneath her. In no time at all, the screaming stopped, and the rapid scramble of mass murder slowed.

"This is the part that's most shocking, Jack. Watch carefully." Major Kingston stated.

There was no need to inform me to watch, for I was already petrified, with my eyes glued to the screen. Fear braided itself into my guts as I watched this Lamian feed on the dead bodies. She sucked them dry, and what's worse, she seemed to be savoring every bite. Each time the sky's lighting would give prospect of the tragedy, a new angle of the serpent came to view. Not only was she feeding off of them, but she was truly enjoying it.

Excitement shot from her eyes, and a constant smile remained implanted on her face. One fang would enter the dead bodies in the upper-chest area, and the second in their stomach. She would suck them dry leaving nothing but skin and bone. After watching this horrendous serpent devour four or five individuals, and then toss them aside as if they were trash, the recording was stopped.

"Now, fast forward again to the blast."

Again, Judy silently followed the Major's instructions. As Judy pressed play, yet again the screen lit up in fire and smoke.

"We sent bombs to the location as soon as we realized the village was under attack. With fire burning strong, the remainder of the recording was watchable without having to rely on the periodic flashes of light from the nights storm. I couldn't believe what was playing out before my eyes. My arms flopped limp to my sides and my jaw dropped open. Everything was on fire. Everything except for the Lamian. She moved through the flames untouched and completely un-bothered. There seemed to be a very thin bluish colored aura around her. It moved and danced atop of her skin and scales in the fire, protecting her from the heat of the flames.

"As you can see, Jackson our fire power is useless."

I continued to watch as she slithered through the flames and out of sight.

"I want to see the video!" Amber shouted from the other apartment.

I looked over at Major Kingston, waiting for him to respond to her demand. His expression remained unchanged. I rolled my eyes as I realized I was the only one who could hear her before I relayed her message.

"Amber wants to see the video."

All three of my guests jumped to their feet in protest. Proclaiming that she wasn't ready, and that showing her the tape would do nothing but cause a panic. Even Judy exclaimed her worry for Amber, stating that if she was to freak out, then The Company would surely shock her yet again. Her body was far too sensitive for more electricity. Did they not realize that she had already over heard the entire recording, as well as the Majors description of it? Did I really need to point out the obvious?

I couldn't believe the tenacity, especially from Judy after I'd grown so instantly fond of her good sense. They'd give Amber more credit and trust if it killed me. We were a team Amber and I, I felt it from the moment I watched her being wheeled helpless down the hallway.

"She already knows, she's been listening in the whole time. I don't see her prancing around causing havoc right now. Do you?" I asked angrily and with heavy sarcasm.

I felt a strong inner pull to Amber. The need to stand up for her overran the need to contain my emotions. As soon as the words escaped my lips, I realized how my intentions could've easily been misconstrued. Surprisingly, the room was silenced. Glances were exchanged back and forth, ultimately resulting in an unspoken agreement with me. Major Kingston gave me a small nod of approval.

"Well?" I said in an average tone, as if speaking to any one of the personnel in my own apartment. "Are you coming over or not?"

Within seconds there was a knock on the door.

Amber was much shiftier, and anxious, than me. She stood by my side the second they walked in. I understood her nerves, and the impossibility of containing them. I'd only been awake for a few hours longer than her, but the difference between then and now was like night and day. Her inability to hold still was clearly affecting everyone there.

More so her own nurse, Brock, than anyone else. His breath was choppy, and his eyes were wide. I rolled my own in response and slipped Amber's fingers into mine. Her skin was smooth and hot. It felt like the warmth of them crawled under my skill, working its way up my arm. It felt right, like a good fit.

"We're in this together." I whispered to her, ever so quietly.

The fidgeting in her deep, dark brown eyes eased up as she stared into mine, confused but surprisingly comforted. She tapped her skinny yet strong fingers against the back of my hand and drummed her heel on the floor. Her lips parted into a small O, as she sucked her breathe in and out focusing on my gaze. Upon letting her head drop down in a few quick nods, I understood it as indication that she was ready. For being so strong and bossy with Brock she seemed to let her guard down with me, and I instantly adored that. My heart leapt. Just holding her hand made me feel more at home than I had since I was ripped away from it.

"Major, play the recording." I respectfully said in control and with confidence, trying to mirror his own proficient mannerisms.

I tucked my insecurities deep inside, refusing to let them to surface. After witnessing the horrendous beast for the first time, I knew that I couldn't let my self-doubts or anxiety show. I had to swallow my personal fear and anguish for the greater good. With Amber's trembling hand clutched into mine, I had a protective surge powering me. I'd keep this woman out of harm's way if my life depended on it. My list of agenda was piling up, along with my consistently growing anger and confusion.

My attention was diverted from the heart wrenching recording I'd already witnessed, to Amber and her reaction to the Lamian. Our hands tightened in grasp. The second time around was just as gruesome and terrifying. One giant tear streamed down Amber's perfectly shaped and delicate cheek. I watched it drip from her chin and absorb into the finely knitted fabric of her gray sweatshirt.

"Oh my God, those poor people."

She whispered under her breath. I watched her closely as an obvious chill ran down her spine. That lone tear was the one and only I'd ever witness Amber shed. With the help of the injection, her heart grew as cold as mine. Together, hand in hand, we formed the bond of a determined team, meant to destroy the greatest of beasts. Amber looked up with eyes as hard as stone.

"How do we kill this bitch?" she asked the Major.

"I'm glad you asked!"

With an upturned grin, and a sparkle of excitement in his eye, he seemed empowered by her question.

"Before you're able to fight this serpent, you need to know everything you possibly can about it. It's getting very late and we're pressed on time. You'll be taught everything we know about this creature. Which, to be quite honest, isn't much. Then you'll watch every camera feed we've caught one on. It's important that you learn how they move. Study how they hide, and how we think they came about. You're being cut down in training time from weeks, to days. The remainder of today will be spent on body and knowledge training all at once. We'll be doubling up on everything, so hopefully the multitask will be manageable as you're adjusting. I wish it could be different, and that we could all take our time, but we can't. Not anymore. Two personal trainers, as well as a Lamain expert instructor, should be here any minute to work with you for the remainder of the night. Any questions?"

Amber and I looked briefly at each other and lied in unison, "No."

"Good. Then tomorrow, bright and early you'll start your military training. It'll be a long day, so eat well and get plenty of rest tonight. We've been tracking these serpents for the past year and now that she's fed, she'll go into hiding. We're estimating it to be anywhere from a couple days to a few weeks before she is ready to feed again. As I said before, this village was large, so she may be full for longer than usual. We'll place you and a small team of soldiers between the village you just witnessed, and our location now. All that we can do is hope she goes for you first. I'm not going to sugar coat things for you. I know this all must be overwhelming, but our future depends on the success of this first mission on the outside, so you need to focus and keep your head."

Major Kingston turned on his heels and headed for the door. No goodbyes or further explanation was intended. Before the door was shut, Amber took a step toward to ask him of the third of us who'd survived the injection. The Major stopped in his tracks and slowly turned to face us. His look was one of puzzlement. His awkward eyebrows were gathered into the center with a crooked wrinkle between them.

"Freddy…" He paused for a few moments before continuing. "Freddy is different. He awoke around the same time as you Amber, but his body has reacted completely different than the two of yours."

"What do you mean by different? And what about the other survivors? The ones of the lesser injection?" I asked.

"Well…" Again, a long pause. "It is hard to say about Freddie, and the other survivors will not be joining us. No one is to know who they are or where, besides The Company. They'll be used for an entirely different purpose. Please direct these questions to doctor Brooklyn, I must be on my way." As quickly as he had dodged the questions, he was out the door.

I listened as he stomped down the hallway and out of ears range. I assumed Amber was listening to his fading footsteps as well because as soon as they were gone she turned her body the same angle as myself at the exact same time. We were moving in unison with each other. I again felt strangely at home in her presence. Our hands were still comfortably clasped together. She shot me a questioning glance, flashed a small portion of her teeth in a catching grin, and then we both turned to face the doctor. As I loosened my grip on her palm to assume my sizable stance, she reacted with a quick squeeze before letting go.

She mocked my position and we stood side by side, with our arms folded across our chests in the same manner my father stood with me on countless occasions. Whether it be because of the same energy pulse that sped through our veins, or whether it was fate, I was continuously drawn to Amber. I could sense that was she to me, too. Together, we were instantly a force to be reckoned with.

Dr. Brooklyn stammered over her words briefly. Her eyes were glued to the two of us, not sure what to make of the situation.

"Um. Uh. Freddy." She started. "Freddy didn't seem to have the energy that the two of you had upon awakening. We're not sure if it's because of the way his body is reacting or if it's because of his life before the injection."

"What do you mean by that?" asked Judy.

She too appeared to be just as curious as Amber and myself. Brock still stood in the corner by the door in wide-eyed silence. Apparently, they'd only been briefed on their own patients, and not of every patient injected.

Dr. Brooklyn kneaded the bottom of her coat nervously. She turned a little more of her attention to Judy as she finished, her beautiful eyes only glanced in Amber and I's direction periodically.

"His living conditions prior to being brought here were very strange. Stranger than any I've seen before, and I'd traveled much with the outside research team for many years before settling in the third division lab permanently."

"Where did he come from?" She asked.

"Well, as you know we can only travel during the day. The lightning makes it too dangerous for the hovercrafts to fly at night. The Company seen Freddy and a few others spread out periodically on the beach line, hunting hogs for years. They never took the life assistance kits that were dropped, rendering us unable to track them. We've still never located their exact sleeping locations. When The Company decided to test their blood, we dropped down for an entire day, and had to net them in order to commence the testing. It is a miracle that one of them actually contained the G-Factor. With only ten people being caught and tested, the odds were one in hundreds."

"Wait a minute." I rudely interrupted. "You're saying that this boy was stalked, netted, held down and forced to give blood, and then pulled away from his family with no warning at all?"

"Well. Yes." Dr. Brooklyn again uncomfortably stammered.

"Typical Company bullshit!" Blurted Amber.

"Now, young lady, it will do you good to hold your tongue!" The doctor scolded with her finger pointed sharply in Amber's face. "You know what happens when you scorn The Company."

This silenced Amber instantly. I noticed the sadness in Amber eyes and wondered what happened to this tortured girl. Dr. Brooklyn looked back at Judy, her demeanor did a complete turnaround. Again, her voice was as uppity and as precise as it'd been the first time I'd met her.

"Aside from his own name, Freddy hasn't spoken a word since he was taken. He went days without food as punishment before the injection, and it never even seemed to bother him. It was as if he was used to hunger, he never budged. He's also been shocked and beaten. They tried to force words out of him on multiple occasions. After a few months in captivity, The Company finally decided to let him eat regularly. They finally stopped the beatings so that his body would be strong enough for the serum."

"How long has he been here?" I asked.

"Almost a year."

"And he hasn't spoken at all?" I continued to prod.

"Not a word." She said.

Dr. Brooklyn continued to explain that upon waking from the injection, Freddy remained speechless and maintained complete body control. He hasn't so much as flinched, aside from the regular sitting and standing he would have normally done. The doctor informed us that Freddy is going to be briefed on the Lamians, just the same as us, whether he shows a reaction or not. He'd also be attending in our training the next day.

I was curious to meet this admirable Freddy. Since I too was raised outside The Company walls, I had deeper appreciation to his reaction. His dedication to silence only sparked a certain level of respect. Amber continued to shift her weight from one foot to the other and occasionally twitch her neck involuntarily at my side as we listened. As the doctor and Judy continued discussing Freddy's strange reaction to the injection, there was a knock on the door.

Seven

After failing to await a friendly greeting, a three-man crew barged in. Two muscular men appearing to be in their early thirties helped themselves into my apartment first. They were followed by an abnormally small young woman who was made it obvious that she wasn't there on her own free will. The men introduced themselves as our personal trainers. Each carried a large pack secured to their backs. They dropped them to the floor, and began to rummage through their goods.

The woman took her place next to the equally uncomfortable Brock in the corner. She waited with a scowl, as the busy men unloaded their bags. They moved furniture in and out of the room with ease. In no time at all the entire room was empty aside from the television, treadmills, and a whole slew of workout equipment that I'd soon become very acquainted with. Dr. Brooklyn quietly excused herself amongst the commotion. Amber and I stood back and observed the men. I tried to wrap my mind around everything that'd happened so far that day, but I was completely incapable.

Both men were of little words. They skipped over any small talk and pleasantries. After presenting themselves as brothers, and as our body improvement coaches, they began first with demonstrations. Upon having the obvious pointed out, it was easy to recognize their similarities as family. The same mannerisms were displayed in the way they moved, the tone of their voices, and even the way their S's and F's were drawn out in speech. Brax, the taller of the two, though only by a fraction of an inch started the explanations first. He took the leadership role between the two of them.

"My name is Brax. This is my brother, Dex. The way we have your workout set up is called a circulatory system. Every ten minutes you'll move from one step to the next. Your focal point will be on this nice young woman, her name is Jess." He pointed to the angry girl as he spoke leaving no time for questions as he continued. "She'll teach you of her knowledge of the outside world and the Lamians. You'll keep your bodies moving while you learn. My brother and I will demonstrate first what you will do at each station. You'll try each one quickly so that we can make sure you are doing each exercise correctly. After which, you'll move around the circulation on your own when indicated by us. You'll listen and learn while moving. Every other workout is arranged in order back and forth between stationary to cardio. We strongly urge you to push yourselves. The Company is curious to test your new capability and limitations. We have little time to see what exactly you can do before you're thrown directly into the field to fight. Therefore, this is your chance to become familiar with your new bodies as well."

The brothers moved from station to station. Starting on the left-hand side was a square mat that was large enough to lay completely down on. This was the stretching station. Dex demonstrated a dozen different stretches to Amber and I, having us practice each one with him before moving to the next station. Jumping rope came easy to Amber, for she had been doing it all her life. I'd never seen or heard of a jump rope and it took me a few tries to work out the rhythm. We moved around the circle, quickly learning of the adjustable hand weights, pull up bars, equalizers, elevation push up blocks, and of course the sturdy and familiar treadmill.

We were allotted a few minutes before beginning, to change our clothes and quickly use the restroom. Before leaving my side, Amber took hold of my hand. The look of fear and confusion in her eyes was apparent, yet she said nothing. She was as lost as me, in this unexpected venture. Parting for even just a few short moments was strangely painful.

It looked like she had so much on her mind, even beyond the injection, and the Lamians. I could tell that she wanted to tell me something, as she searched my eyes, but she couldn't find the words. I too wanted nothing more than to speak with someone who I actually cared about, someone who truly cared about me.

I wanted to tell her about my father. I wanted to hold her tight and take her pain away. Neither of us would ever be able to truly tell each other our deepest innermost thoughts and feelings without the prying ears of The Company. This simple fact only fueled my hate to them. Amber would never confide in me unconditionally, nor I in her. Yet another deeply inflicted wound caused by The Company.

After locking eyes in an understood and unspoken moment, Amber and I momentary parted. I made my way to the kitchen first, and fetched a much needed drink of water. I was thirstier than I realized. With the adrenalin still rushing through me, I'd hardly noticed the dry knot in my throat. One glass after another of ice-cold water sloshed through my mouth and down my neck. The chill of it felt astonishing as it cooled the burn inside my chest and stomach. I couldn't get enough.

Then, after relieving myself quickly. I had only a few moments to change my clothing. Judy explained the works of my dressers and closet. Opting for airy shorts, rather than the hot sweatpants seemed appropriate. I ultimately decided against a shirt. I'd spent most of my life without one and this strange new body heat was radiating from me, I didn't want to trap it in. A few dozen tops hung loosely in my closet. I wondered what need any one person could possibly have for such an unnecessary collection. I blew off the pointless thought, and I left the pointless attire to hang unworn.

Amber must've been moving just as quickly as I. Possibly even quicker. Just as I made my way back into the living room she came bounding through the door. Brock, as always, was two steps behind her. He followed her like a pet whose master had no need for him. As if he was begging for her attention, only to be brushed off and pushed aside. She rudely and purposely ignored his presence.

My jaw dropped at the sight of her. Her hair was pulled back and messy on the back of her head, exposing her neck and jaw line completely. With flawless pores and perfect skin pigment, much like my own, she was astonishing. She wore a thin white top, showing off her perfectly sculpted abs, and exercise shorts exposing her tone legs. She moved with a certain athletic grace that's completely indescribable. Brax and Dex, were nearly drooling all over themselves at the sight of her. I instinctively growled under my breath.

Amber looked around at us all in the room. All of us that were all staring bluntly in her direction.

"Well, are we going to do this or what?" She demanded, annoyed and completely in control.

The mumbles, stutters, and the clearing of guilty throats cut through the air. We were busted. I couldn't help but smile. I didn't care one bit that I'd been staring, she was beautiful, and my eyes held their purposeful gaze. As our embarrassed trainers averted their attention and searched for words, Amber turned her attention to me.

"What are you smiling at, Mister Bellony?" She asked with booming sarcasm. There were no words. My grin only widened, consuming the larger portion of my face, I'm sure.

Jess, the quiet girl who'd been patiently waiting in the back of the room, stepped forward and demanded our attention. I was surprised at her ability to capture and hold our ambience the way she did. She'd been so quiet up until now. So petite, seemingly shy and insecure. I couldn't have been more wrong. Jess, the tiny girl in the quiet corner who now demanded respect in such a manner that she'll forever stand out in memory.

"Everybody shut your mouths, take your places, and listen!" Her voice carried, and her eyes glossed over.

She tossed Amber and I each a hand full of the same small sticky devices that we'd used several times. Jess didn't tell us what to do with them. She only folded her arms and lifted a brow, while she tapped her foot impatiently waiting for us to put them on. Jess stood tall and let out an angry sigh. We quickly placed the devices on our heads and chests, and then took our places in the workout circulation.

I started with the familiar, and I began running on the treadmill. Amber went straight for a jump rope. As we began pushing our bodies, Jess diverted her demanding expression to Brax.

"Start your timers, boys. I don't want any interruptions from the two of you, other than your whistles letting them know when to move, do I make myself clear?"

They mumbled their agreements allowing Jess to continue. She dimmed the lights and let her fingers go to work on a small tablet, much like Judy's. The television again came to life, and it was just as quickly paused.

"You'll keep your eyes on me at all times unless you are told otherwise. You may ask questions pertaining to the discussion, and only to the discussion. Don't be afraid to ask, because we need you to be as educated as possible. It's important that you know and understand what you're going up against, but keep your bodies moving!"

Jess again put herself to work on the tablet for a few moments before continuing. I ran as fast as my legs would allow. Faster and faster they moved beneath me. The motion was empowering. It felt good to release my roaring energy. Though Judy, Dex, Brax and Brock strained and struggled to pay attention over the top of Amber and I's running and jumping, we had no trouble. We were still able to hear every detail of everything around. I retained each word of our following discussion… every single word. I can only assume Amber did as well.

"It is my understanding that the Major showed you the video of last night's attack at a village, not too far from here. As he may have told you, she is the largest Lamian we have seen yet. I'm here to show you others. Together we'll study the ways they move, their speed, and of course their history. We don't know much about where they came from, and we don't know how many are. Had either of you heard of this creature before today?" She asked. Amber and I each nodded our heads. "Well then, let's hear what you know. You first princess." She said, and then glared at Amber.

Amber clearly didn't appreciate the princess comment. She glared right back, lowering her lids to a mere slit. Her lips formed into a thin line, and the blood vein in her neck revealed her quickening pulse. I could feel the anger fill the room, and all but see the hate filling up in her chest. Again, a small grin began to form on my face, I couldn't help it.

"It's Amber, not princess. And I don't know anything more about them than what the Major showed us. All that I'd heard before today, was that they existed. You know as well as me that The Company keeps *anything* worth knowing a secret!" Amber exaggerated the last sentence in clear defiance.

Jess held her glare uncompromised, then turned her attention to me.

"And you, Jackson?"

"I heard a story of where they might have originated, but I don't know how true it is."

"Enlighten us, Caveman."

I was able to blow off Jess's rude name calling much easier than Amber. I only chuckled and then continued my explanation. I seasoned it with only the necessary facts, and I left out as much as I could about Johnson and my village.

"I heard that there was an original serpent thousands of years ago, and her name was Lamia. I guess the Gods made her into this creature as punishment, and when she died there were unborn snakes inside of her. I heard that the lightning carried magic from the Gods that awakened them."

I watched Jess' face change from stern to ponder. The frown wrinkles at the corners of her mouth smoothed, and the downward pull of her brows lifted. It only lasted a moment, though, because as soon as chuckles came from Dex and Brax behind me her face instantly dropped back to its previous expression.

"Silence!" Jess cussed. "Don't the two of you have a job to be doing?"

Just as she pointed it out, Dex blew into the silver instrument he called a whistle, that was hanging around his neck. As the loud, high pitched squeal sounded, we moved into the next workout in the circulation. I picked up the weights, adjusted them quickly to the max limit, and began curling them with ease. I bent my arms at the elbow, and with a straight back I lifted them from my legs to chest. The muscles in my arms bulged and my breath remained steady and unchallenged. I quickly glanced at Amber who was pulling herself up and down on the pull up bar with no trouble at all. She looked back at me with a proud smirk. She too was impressed with our new-found strength.

"Pay attention!" Jess again overpowered. "I knew this whole workout while learning process would be a distraction." She shook her head and let out a long-winded sigh. "Oh well, I suppose it is necessary."

Before pressing me for more information on my own knowledge of the Lamians, she observed us with a hint of surprise as well. Surely, she was taking in the amount of weight I was lifting with such ease and Amber's ability to pull her body weight over and over without a struggle.

"Where did you hear this, Jack?" She finally asked.

I quickly fabricated a lie in effort to protect Johnson.

"A drifter passed through my village. It a couple years before I was brought here."

I assumed that by embellishing a time frame, and underplaying the trauma of being taken, The Company would have no suspicions.

"I'm not sure who he was or where he came from. That's why I don't know how much of its true. He said that he had traveled far and that he had spoken to people first hand who knew of the serpent's destruction personally. He said that the story came from much study, and was being passed along to warn the people that they were coming. He also said that descendant snakes of the original Lamia, bite only the most beautiful women and that it takes them years to change into the creature."

Jess thought deeply of what I had said. "That actually plays out very similar to our own knowledge of the Lamians." She acknowledged, and scratched at the crown of her head. "The Company found several old documents dating back centuries before the storm began. They too spoke of this cursed woman and her myth. Olden time books state that it was in fact just a myth. An ancient belief, said to be originated in the beginning of human kind."

Jess continued to ponder for some time as her fingers again went to work on the tablet. A solid unmoving picture of a black and white sketched version of the creature popped up on the television. Before Jess explained the drawing, Dax blew his whistle. With no comments or following remarks, Amber and I moved to our next stations and Jess continued.

"This is a picture found by The Company, it dates back the furthest. It's said to be of the original serpent, Lamia."

The darkly shaded scales on the woman warped into her long thickly coiled serpent half. Her fangs were just as long as the new age Lamian that had been caught on camera the night before. Jess pressed another button and the screen split in two separate pictures side by side.

"The picture on the left is the first creature we were able to catch on camera. This was taken nearly five years ago on the other side of our continent."

The second picture was in color, yet shaded by the darkness of night, with a crack of lightning in the background. The similarities were breathtaking. Each Lamian held their arms at their sides, slightly bent back. Their heads were tilted to the right allowing them to look out of the tops of their sharp eyes with a matching evil glint… They looked excited. Even their serpent halves were coiled back and forth in parallel curves, bending and curling in exact proportions. The two were nearly identical.

"The Company is not aware of any story explaining how this creature has been reincarnated or multiplied. I suppose there are several myths out there, but until we have any kind of valid proof we'll stick with exactly what we know. This tale you heard, Jackson, about the unborn snakes brought to life by the Gods, could possibly be true, yet it may not. There's no way to tell for an absolute, therefore it'll do you good to keep that bit of information to yourself from here on out."

I couldn't agree with her more. We watched several slides of the progression in the serpents. They grew in size and number; the pictures and videos were overwhelming. Together, we studied the movement in the creature's scales. The position she coiled herself into, just before striking, was very distinct. Though we were limited on views and angles due to the darkness, so we worked with what we had. We learned her movements as best as possible.

After studying the creature, we moved onto the land. The forest I grew up in was sparse, yet still considered a forest. The first Lamian we were to hunt was in a much vaster terrain. The entire place was made up of sand and hills. This all looked so much different than the dirt and mud I was used to. There was little to no vegetation. The local people who'd been viciously torn apart by the beast, had lived off very little. We learned that they ate mostly lizards, turtles, and an occasional rabbit or coyote. They had wells dug out of the sand for water and depended on cactus to survive when the wells ran dry. This would be yet another giant adjustment for me in lifestyle. Hopefully we wouldn't have to stay out in it for too long.

Time flew by as we pushed our bodies and learned. After announcing that we'd been working for over three hours, Jess decided to call it a night. She bid us good luck, urging us to get plenty of rest, for tomorrow would be a big day of training. I wasn't tired in the slightest. After everything I'd watched, I knew there was no way I'd be able to sleep. That's not to mention the energy that was still spewing from the pit of my body. I looked over at Amber, who appeared to remain just as anxious as myself. After being pushed aside by Brax and Dex as they gathered their equipment, Amber stood again at my side and took my hand into hers.

She looked back at Judy and Brock before announcing, "We're going for a walk."

Judy, who had pulled a kitchen chair into the room and had been quietly snacking and observing along with Brock, jumped to her feet.

"I. I. I don't think that is such a good idea!"

Brock slowly stood next to her in an exhausted agreement. Apparently, watching us running and lifting had made *him* tired. I chuckled in my head at the thought. I wondered if randomly going for a walk in The Company was a normal thing. I thought back to home and remembered the relaxing trails and quiet riverbank that I missed so much. I closed my eyes and took a wiff, willing myself to smell the scent of spruce. All that filled my nostrils was the scent of sweat, along with a pinch of left over garlic from the bread I'd ate earlier.

"Don't worry about us, really. I promise we won't go far. And besides." Amber pointed up to the camera in the corner of the room, and then slowly and deliberately at her own head. "Do you really think we could get into much mischief without being found, or punished for that matter?"

She had a valid point and our nurses knew it. Judy looked at us with much concern, and she stood blocking the doorway to the hall with her feet planted firm. No sooner than she could agree or not, the telephone rang. Judy pulled it from her jacket pocket, pressed a button, and held it to her ear. I could hear the same old demanding man's voice as the last time she spoke into that annoying device.

"Let them go." He insisted, and then hung up his end before she had a chance to respond.

Amber let out a mocking chuckle and then mumbled under her breath so only I, and The Company of course, could hear, "Typical," she smirked. She then pulled me out of the apartment and into the hallway, leaving our nurses to their own business, and our coaches to finish packing their gear.

Walking hand in hand with Amber was comfortable and somewhat relaxing. I could feel the heat pulsing out of her body, as was my own. I searched for the right words to say and the proper discussion to start with. There was so much that needed to be said between both of us. I was grateful that she started the conversation, and even more grateful that it was a personal one.

"So, do you have any family, Jack?" she asked.

I told her about my father and how I was taken. I was fully aware that The Company was listening, but at that moment I didn't care. They knew what they'd done to me. There was no hiding anything or holding back. I expected to hear soldier's boots, stomping in our direction to stop the conversation, but there was nothing.

We drowned out the sounds of the people behind the doors we were passing with conversation of our own. Not caring about their lives or current situations. Amber and I were completely together in the moment. It was everything I'd needed since the day I was forced into The Company walls.

She told me about her family and about how they too were taken from her by The Company, but the situation was completely different. Amber grew up with both of her parents. They had a strong bond and held together a very close family. Amber had an older sister as well. They were only a few years apart in age and best friends their entire lives. Up until the day that The Company's men barged in and murdered her family in cold blood. All aside from Amber.

The Company knew that her blood was rich with the G-Factor. They'd been keeping a close watch on her for some time. Amber told me of how her mother and father had started a conspiracy against The Company. They worked in the food and supply section, which happened to be in separate towers on the opposite end of The Company walls. I was astonished to hear of how many buildings and lifestyles were formed here. Amber told me of how her parents started a food storage and preparation, hiding it from The Company little at a time.

They spoke of how The Company was divided from within, and that someday there'd be a war within the walls. The Company heard of this outrageous display of defiance. They stormed into her family's apartment, and they shot them all in their sleep. From there, Amber was taken to the third division section to await her injection.

Like me, Amber hadn't spoken to anyone about her family's tragedy until now. She was continuously pausing and stopping to listen for the running of boots just the same as I was. We both knew that we'd be able to hear them coming long before we ever saw them. They never came. We wondered aloud why they hadn't stopped our conversation and agreed that they needed us now more than ever. We assumed that The Company was allowing us to grow close so that we could work better together. After making our way up and down, weaving from hall to hall, we turned around to make our way back to the apartments.

Though never truly alone, this was the closest thing to alone time I'd had with Amber. It was a moment of solace. Our conversation was tragic and full of devastation, yet unexpectedly healing. It was reassuring to talk openly of my father. It'd been over a month now, since I walked in the comfort of his presence, or heard the wisdom in his words. After talking about him and explaining him to Amber, for the first time, I could feel him inside of me. His strength resigned in my heart. His intuition surged through my thoughts. I could even feel the sureness of his hands in my own as I held onto hers tightly. I needed that. I needed him, and more importantly… I needed Amber.

Eight

After enjoying a scrumptious meal, Amber and I parted ways. This time it was for the entire night, and it was even harder to pull away from her. Though we could still keep tabs on each other through the walls, my stomach churned as I watched her exit my apartment. Judy shoved a couple of tiny blue pills into my palm. She insisted that I take them to help calm my still apparent nerves. She said it would relax my body, allowing me to slip into a much-needed sleep, or "reboot" as she called it.

I swallowed them with ease and without question. Within seconds of feeling them slide down my throat, my body slipped into a strange state of relaxation. My arms instantly dropped to my sides and my eye lids began to droop. I lifted my heavy legs in a slow stride, walking right to my room. My head hit the pillow and instantaneously I was out. Darkness consumed me as I fell into an uninterrupted, and dreamless sleep.

I woke the next morning with a giant stretch. Refreshed and energized, I jumped out of bed with ease. I felt fantastic! Either the adrenalin had slowed, or I'd become accustomed to it. No matter the case, it was amazing. The scratching hum of Judy's unmistakable snore was echoing throughout the apartment. I recalled Major Kingston stating that we'd have an early start.

I made a mental note to have the workings of time, and clocks, explained to me in full as soon as possible. This not knowing was getting old fast. There was no need to learn the details of time back home. We counted the days by lining stones against our cave walls. That's all that was needed. I was learning fast that The Company worked in deeper time-oriented detail. The less I knew about the ways of the people in The Company, the more insecure it made me. All that I could do now was push forward to learn their ways.

I took advantage of the moment and helped myself to another refreshing shower. It was equally as fantastic as the first. As I stood under the pressurized water, I wondered what lay ahead. I pictured the Lamain serpent I'd soon be fighting, and I prayed for help. I imagined her vicious fangs sinking into Amber, and I shuddered. I'd need to focus now more than ever. A day of concentration and perseverance lay ahead, and I had to get my head right.

My body seemed to run even hotter that it had the day before. I turned the dial on the water tap, cooling it to a lower temperature. The cold water was astonishing. Upon hearing a rustling around in the other room, I decided to leave the much-appreciated shower behind and face the inevitable day that lay ahead.

I shoveled down my breakfast quickly upon Judy's instruction. As I finished my meal and dressed I listened to Amber shout orders at Brock. I giggled out loud, which she must have picked up on because as soon as the chuckle came out, she turned her attention to me.

"Stop laughing at me, Jackson Bellony!"

I only laughed harder. The amusement continued as I swallowed the last bite of my toast and eggs. I made my way to the unnecessarily huge closet in my room, and then slipped into a strangely comfortable pair of jeans. I was impressed with the feel of them compared to the leather I was used to, I looked myself over in the mirror at my side. I bent at the waist and knees trying them out. It was a nice surprise. Was it possible for my arms to be even bigger? I flexed them, one quick time to confirm. Astonishing! This might not be so bad after all. My grin widened as I looked myself over from every angle. I pulled one of the plain black shirts over my head just in time to hear Judy.

"Are you ready, Jack? We don't want to keep the Major waiting. Those military men don't handle tardiness very well."

Together, the four of us rushed from one end of the Third Division West Wing to the other. We stepped into a metal box that they explained to me as being an elevator. I couldn't help but grab onto a bar that was secured in place behind me as I felt the ground move beneath my feet. Amber chuckled at me, just the same as I had her a few minutes earlier while eves dropping. I shot her a look of warning and quickly shook it off. I'd rather her joke and be playful about my ignorance than annoyed. A loud *ding*, rang through my ears and the doors slid open in front of me. I felt my eyes widen, and my grip tighten around the bar I was clutching.

As the light between the sliding elevator doors expanded before me, so did my view. Lights, buildings, towers, and people. I was overwhelmed! My heart sunk to the soles of my shoes. I gasped in shock of the thousands of people. The largest existing city was instantly displayed in front of me. It was alive, and it moved in waves. There were no trees, nor hills, or even water. When Amber had told me that the food supply was artificially created in a building, I wasn't sure what to expect, but I do know this wasn't it. A giant, clear, see through tube surrounded us and led from our elevator to the next building over. I held my breath as I looked down, unable to step away from the comfort of the moving metal box.

"It's only ten stories down Jack, that's not so bad." Amber encouraged.

"Not bad?"

"Nope, not at all." Her grin widened, lifting her ears and her cheeks simultaneously. She laces her fingers into mine and pulled me into the tube.

I moved with caution. I carefully placed one foot in front of the other, as lightly as possible, tiptoeing my way inside. Afraid I would fall through the glass beneath me, I held my breath. It felt as if I was walking on air. How was everyone so comfortable with this?

I looked around at the hundreds of people rustling through similar glass tubes from building to building. I didn't seem to faze any of them. We moved through thin, muggy air on glass that was hardly even apparent. The Company wall was enormous, and it seemed to never end on either side of us. Stretching for miles and standing taller than even the tallest towers, it surrounded the buildings and engulfed us in a protective rock structure. It was beautiful, yet at the same time utterly suffocating.

Below me were more glass tubes of people. Below that was the rush of trains and buses. I'd read of such things many times, but again they were far from what I pictured them to be. Though we were looking down from such a height, my vision was impeccable. I could see each person rushing back and forth. I could see the details of the bus roofs, and the rails for the trains to move un in perfect detail. The view was astonishing and completely unbelievable. After getting used to the strange see through, yet solid footing, I relaxed my stride and absorbed my surroundings.

I later learned that when the wall had first been built, it stretched far beyond the buildings of The Company, reaching near the outer limits of the liquid energy underground. Everything inside the liquid area was protected from the lightning, leaving plenty of room for growth. Since then, The Company has more than *just* grown. It's continuously packed in more and more material, delivered everyday by The Company workers and their constantly moving hovercrafts. In shift work, the buildings were erected back to back, so close together that there's hardly even any room to breathe.

Most people living within The Company has never seen so much as a pond or a brush. Oh, was Amber in for a treat, I thought. I couldn't wait to get away from this strange, crowded, lit up and impersonal place. I imagined myself to be in the woods and amongst the trees as I moved ever so cautiously to the next building.

As we reached the end of the glass tube, a new elevator, in a new building, awaited our arrival. The movement of this elevator was a bit more expected and a little less startling as the last. My anticipation was much stronger than the tiny flutter in my stomach. We quickly moved through two more buildings and two more floating glass extensions before we reached the military tower. It was one of the tallest buildings of The Company. Men wearing the same unnerving black suits as the one's who'd taken me from my father were everywhere. They lined the hallway guarding each door. They marched in unison and looked ahead as if we were nonexistent. With every black suit I passed, my anger grew.

I searched the faces for anyone who was involved in the so-called medical testing that resulted in the separation from my home. Not one man or woman looked familiar. I held my head high and kept a straight face, but inside my blood was boiling. With teeth clenched tightly and fists balled at my sides, I repeated in my head a silent encouragement to keep composure.

Major Kingston was waiting in front of a giant metal door. It was much different than any of the others. I was starting to become accustomed to being thrown into the unknown. What could be awaiting behind this door that is possibly any worse than anything I had seen or been put through so far? In merely one month, every detail of my life had changed, and my body for that matter. All changes that were forced upon me and unwelcome.

The Major's stern face, or the intimidating metal door, held no sense of urgency or fear for me. I stood stronger with every passing moment. I was ready to move forward, knowing that the sooner we were finished here, the sooner I could be outside of The Company walls. I wanted to feel the earth beneath my feet and fresh clean air in my lungs. I'd fight any creature for that luxury. At that moment, I began to channel the ever building anger, I was determined to use it in my tasks ahead. I'd flip my hate for The Company against the bigger and more urgent enemy, the Lamians.

"Well, Well, I'm glad you could finally make it." The Major said as he glared at Judy and Brock. He waived his wrist in front of the small box on the wall next to the door, then pushed it open with little effort. "Follow me." He mumbled under his breath.

Taking the leadership roll between the four of us, I followed Major Kingston into the training room first. The smell of fresh sweat lingered in the air and filled my nostrils. Sounds of clanking metal, choppy breaths, and squeaking springs echoed in my enhanced ear drums. Hot air smothered me, heightening my already burning pores, and instantly watering my eyes. The door shut behind us with a loud *clank*. Just inside the door, we stood in the shape of moving geese. A 'V' with the Major at the tip of our triangle, Amber and I at his flanks, and our nurses behind each of us, never leaving arm's length. In front of us were dozens of men and women in a giant open room. We were surrounded by cement walls and slightly padded floors.

A small grin formed across the Major's face as he allowed us to absorb our surroundings. He waited a few moments before he began to explain. The training men and women were working in teams of two and four. Across the edges of the room, they were jumping high into the air doing all different kinds of flips, turns, kicks and lunges. In the furthest corner were knives, axes, and arrows being flung in every direction. Directly in front of us, only a couple yards away, were two extremely large men in pads and suits. They held long, dark, thick blades in each hand. The weapons were sharp enough for the light to throw sparks from their edges. I watched in awe as they swung them at one another, stopping and dodging each other's blows.

"This is your new classroom." The Major explained. "And these men and women are your teachers. From what I understand, you'll be able to learn and retain more from watching than most people are able learn from years of training. I want you to separate, observe, and practice what they teach you. After your morning of training here, we'll be going to the village that was attacked. Then we'll find a place to camp, in wait of the Lamain. You'll learn of the habitat, and become familiar with the camps surroundings. You two, along with Freddy."

The Major paused and looked down at his watch. "Who is also late." He shook his head in disgust then continued. "We'll take a little nap before the dark settles in and the lightning begins. You'll need to be refreshed and awake during the night. You'll stay at camp, along with a small army, until she shows up. There's no way to tell how long that may take. Now if you will excuse me I must wait for Freddy."

The Major turned on his heels and marched back through the metal door, leaving us to ourselves. Amber and I glanced at each other quickly. Her smile grew and I could sense the excitement in her eyes.

"I'm going for the trampoline first!" She took off in a giddy sprint to the back wall.

"What is a trampoline?" I mumbled the question quietly, and a little embarrassed.

Judy stepped forward taking over Amber's now empty space at my side. "You see how high they're jumping?"

"Yes"

"That's because they're bouncing on trampolines. My guess is that it's helping them learn how to flip their bodies and get accustomed with certain movements before they're preformed on solid ground. What do you want to learn first, Jack?"

"That."

I pointed directly ahead at the large men with swinging, sparking blades. Judy only stayed by my side momentarily. Her eyes burned a hole in the ground at our feet. She was clearly just as uncomfortable as she was scared. As I started circling the pair watching each movement, she walked away. She made herself unseen along with Brock, hiding out in the corner, no doubt. I didn't care enough to look or pay attention to our nurses.

I was mesmerized. Sparks flew every which way as the metal blades crashed into each other. I watched the angles of each man's arms and their legs with each lunge and swing. I memorized the way their bodies moved up and down, spinning to their sides, kneeling and twisting. I calculated every minuscule shoulder-to-wrist movement.

After a while of constantly moving and dodging, the smaller of the two men had the other pinned to the ground with the blade to his neck. They nodded at each other as a sign of defeat before the man on the ground was helped to his feet by the other. The victor of the two turned to face me while the looser began stripping off his pads. He dropped the material at my feet and marched away.

"Put these on." The victor demanded.

I'd watched the order they were stripped off from the other man. It put them on myself in the same fashion, without argument or struggle. The pads were soon secured around my arms and legs. Everything was made of a strange, slick, light weight material. I could bend and move with ease. He then handed me a blade. The man jumped right into a training session. No need for small talk or introductions. He was wise, skilled and spoke with direction.

"Feel the metal." Holding his blade out to me he spoke rigorously.

I pulled my hand away instantly, looking angrily at the frozen burn on my fingertips.

"It's freezing!"

"Yes. It's made with a special steal. As was shown to you yesterday, the Lamians can withstand fire. Heat, and the debris from our bombs bounce off them as if they have some sort of force field."

"Force field?"

"Yes, it's like a protective layer surrounding them. We have no way to tell how much is blocked by this protection, but we're taking all possible precautions. We know that she can move through fire, so we're hoping that temperatures in the extreme opposite will penetrate her. The throwing knives and arrow tips are made with similar material. Now, I assume you've been watching and calculating our movements. Am I right?"

"Yes, of course."

"Well, then let's get started."

He picked up the second blade that'd been left behind from his previous sparring partner. He threw it with ease into my throbbing hand. I grabbed the handle fast and without hesitation. My reflexes were phenomenal, and I was surprisingly comfortable holding the deadly weapon.

I bent at the knees in a mocking fashion, parallel to his. I held my arms in the same position. One arm I held strongly in front of me in an offensive position, and the other at my side, ready to strike. Without an explanation the man lunged towards me, blade first. I moved quickly, blocking his blow with ease. Icey sparks flew, and my mind raced. As if everything else around me was in slow motion, I was able to recall and calculate each movement that I had absorbed, while watching this man in his last fight. I dropped to my knees and rolled towards him.

I took him out at the legs and blocked the offensive strike he threw while falling. He hit the ground instantly, making a loud *thud* as his shoulders collided into the padded mat on the floor. Not allowing him time to roll away from my grasp, I touched my blade to his neck, just as he had done. The tip of it left a little red burn, just above his Adam's apple. I held my stance strong, pressing just hard enough to indent and burn the skin, without slicing it open. How was I able to move so precisely? I knew exactly what I was doing. My body mimicked the man sparing before me, only quicker and calculated to the exact detail. I felt empowered and self-assured.

Taken by surprise, the man stood with uncertainty in his eyes. He assumed the starting position. His feet moved with skill as he began circling. I could practically see the wheels turning in his head as be debated on whether to make the first move. Focused and with a steady hand, I again ran everything I had witnessed through my head. I recalled a few distinctive jumps and lunges that I was anxious to try while observing.

I jumped into the air with my body tilted, spinning to the right I pushed each blade towards him mid twist. Spinning in a complete circle through the air the sparks from his offensive blocks flew high. As my feet again touched the ground, my arms instantly contracted in short yet powerful angles. The man charged me, at full me. He wasn't holding back in the slightest. He was skilled and ready for the fight.

The man had clearly been holding back the first round, testing me, and he likely wasn't pleased about getting caught by surprise. He was now determined, and driven by his embarrassment over the quick take down. Swinging, kneeling, and twisting, the man's defense was nearly overwhelming. My speedy, magnified sight calculated the moves coming from his core and shoulders as he pushed forward. In that moment, for me, it was defense... strictly defense. I dodged and blocked each of his blows as he charged. I needed to turn this around and fast.

I watched his face and felt the power of his swings decrease. This giant man was tiring. I quickly determined that this was his weakness. Rather than falling back in steps while blocking his powerful blows I began pushing forward. Though still on the angry defense he was now being forced to strain his tired arms. Upon feeling his increasingly weakened and slowing state, I tried a new move. A move that was all my own.

I shifted on my feet in one quick unexpected motion. He was unable to defend himself as I held the blades above my head in the shape of an X, leaned my body down, tilting forward, and charged him with my head and shoulders. By grabbing one of his own blades between the two of mine, he was unable to move it. I then used the three blades together to block his free shoulder moving completely underneath his final swing. The motion knocked him to the ground.

I landed on his chest and rolled myself forward over the top of him. I used the crossed blades to completely disarm him, all the while using the weight of my knee to push the air from his lungs. I quickly stood proud and victorious with one blade again pressed to his neck and the other firmly over his heart.

A defeated nod was managed by my surprised opponent. I released my hold and allowed him to stand. His chest rose and fell deeply, as he struggled to his feet. My heart continued to beat at the same pace, breath remained at ease, and my hands were continuously steady. As he stood, I realized that the once distracting sounds from the rest of the room had stilled. I was in such focus and concentration that I hadn't realized our audience.

The room was quiet, and all eyes were staring in our direction. A circle had formed around us. An applaud was started by Major Kingston in the back of the crowd, and it instantly grew. I scanned the faces with a humbled pride. One man stood out. He was the only guy in the room aside from me, to be wearing jeans and a t-shirt. His skin tone and pigment were perfected, exactly like Amber's and my own. His arms remained folded across his chest and his face cold. He looked to be a little older than me, yet strong. Much more muscular than myself. A large scar ran from beneath his ear, down his neck and disappeared into the top of his shirt. He didn't appear to be fazed, or even impressed. I assumed him to be Freddy.

The man pushed his way past the cheering crowd, who again silenced when he reached the center of their circle. Without a word, he looked back and forth between me and the man I'd just defeated. He held my gaze for a few seconds before speaking. It was the first words he'd broken since he had been taken by The Company. Over a year of silence, and it finally ended. History was made as his lips parted. Gasps broke through the air and he held the attention of every unblinking eye.

"Mind if I try?"

His voice was deep, and the question lingered in the quiet room. The defeated man silently stripped himself of his padding, and let it drop heavily on the cement. Freddy kicked the padding aside, and held out his hands for the blades, all the while holding eye contact with myself. He was confident and intimidating. He'd clearly been watching and calculating movements just as I had before, taking on the task first hand. Fearlessly, Freddy meant business.

He took a blade in each hand and began backing away from me. The crowd parted as he continued to back up. Further and further he moved, holding eye contact the whole time. I stood in wonder as I watched him move all the way to the edge of the training room. The space was big, yet I could still see him in perfect detail. As he came to an abrupt halt, a mischievous smile formed slyly across his face. He opened his mouth to speak.

The crowd leaned in and strained to hear. Of course, Amber, I, and the eaves-dropping Company men, were the only ones who held the privilege of hearing his quiet instruction.

"She'll be coming from far away, and fast. She's powerful. Much more so than that idiot you just took down. If we actually expect to kill her, we're going to have to train each other and work together. No more of this separate and observe nonsense. We need to know what each other is bringing to the fight. We need to learn the way each other moves, so that we can use our strengths against her as a team. She may not have blades to fight with, but her claws are just as sharp. Her scales and fangs are deadly. We can't depend on The Company to teach us survival. This is completely on us. I'm not sure about you, but I have a lot to protect. And, a lot to live for. If today is our only day of training, I need to know that you're ready to fight with me."

Freddy was wise. My stomach turned as his words of wisdom bounced around my mind. He was right, and painfully so. Since the day before when I watched the video of the beast, I'd been depending on The Company completely without even realizing it. It took this very moment to reach into myself and find true understanding of the situation. It hit me as strong as a bolt of the familiar lightning. His words stuck me right at the core. This was as real as it could get. Life or death.

"I'm ready." I whispered back.

Freddy came at me. His speed was impressive. Within seconds he cleared the length of the room. The rest of the people moved to the edges, giving us all the space possible. Anticipation was thick in the crowd. Freddy was instantly before me, with metal swinging from every angle. As I stomped and lunged in his direction, he bounced from one foot to the other, moving his body with ease on either side of my blades. He moved completely untouched. He dropped his blades, picked up my body by the neck and one thigh, and then threw me backward with what felt like the force of the almighty.

He was just as strong as he looked. I flew through the air, my blades dropping next to his on the cement's padding. I hit the floor with a *thud* and skidded back several feet. I stood quickly, I ran back toward him. I'd give this fight everything I had. I was determined. He may've been strong, but so was I. My father's face flashed before my eyes. Live or die, I thought.

Coming up fast Freddy, was crouched down with one blade rather than two. Just as I approached I dropped to my right hip, using the momentum to slide across the floor. I grabbed both of my weapons as I moved. I rolled toward his feet, swinging with unexplainable speed and grace. My weapons and body moved as one. It was comfortable, it felt as natural chewing food. I looked up at Freddy as I moved across the floor, only to be taken by astonishment at his own new moves.

As if in slow motion I watched and calculated his spin. Within inches of myself, he lept from his crouched position and spun through the air perfectly, dodging my blade entirely. He sucked in his unprotected stomach. The insanely sharp edge of my blade sliced through the fabric of his shirt, exposing his muscular core. The crowd gasped and squealed. With as much energy as we had in the beginning, we continued to move, never stopping or pausing. There was no need to regroup or to catch our breath.

We took turns in the attack, neither of us leaving the other any room for hesitation. We learned from each other's movements, and we pushed forward, using the entire training room in our dedicated practice. After several life-threatening blocks and dodges, I was finally able to unexpectedly pin Freddie to the ground. Again, the crowd responded.

Freddy stood, and looked me in the eye. The largest smile I'd ever seen filled his cheeks.

"I'm Freddy." He finally said, confidently. He held out his hand and I shook it proudly.

"Jack." I said in return.

"You chose a great start for training. It'll be an honor to fight with you. As I was saying before there hasn't been a soul around that's been worth my time until now. I've met one of these creatures before." He pointed to the scar on his neck. "Even the injection was unable to fix her damages. The important thing is that I lived. We can learn more from each other than we can anyone else. With our new speed, strength, and weapons, I know we can defeat her as a team."

"How did you get away?"

"It doesn't matter now." He scowled at the floor. "The location we'll be in is different than my home."

"Mine too."

"We'll have to learn our surroundings quickly. Lucky for The Company, you were raised outside their walls as a hunter, and I as a fighter. I've been trained my entire life in the things they are teaching here." Freddy averted his attention to Amber. He looked past The Companies military men as if they were nonexistent. "You're just as strong, and as smart as the two of us. I have only one question for you. Are you as brave? Or will you freeze up when the time comes to fight?"

"Excuse me?" She demanded.

"You can learn a lot about a person when they're thrown into battle."

Anger swept Amber's face. Her foot steps were heavy as she marched toward us. With one quick motion she swiped the blade from my hand and swung. Flinging the tip until it stopped abruptly at Freddy's unprotected neck, indenting the skin just so. Fearless eyes burned on each of their face, and within seconds the scrapping began. I stood back proudly and absorbed from within the crowd. From one end of the training room to the other they moved. Their bodes spun in skilled movements. Sparks flew high and rapidly. Not that I needed the reassurance, I already knew that Amber could hold her own. If I hadn't known otherwise, I would've thought her to have been training for years.

After the sparring deceased we moved onto other things. The crowd of impressed military men resumed their own routines and expertise. They taught and demonstrated as we moved from station to station. We learned together as a three-man team. We practiced, and quickly mastered each task presented. Knife and axe throwing were amongst the easiest for each of us. For me, it was merely a thrilling talent. I'd been hunting with bows, traps, and knives my entire life. I was already very familiar with them.

For Amber, knife throwing seemed to be her calling. She was deadly, and perfectly accurate. Our magnified sight allowed the targets to stand out. Our increasingly calculated movements, muscle memory, and overall retention allowed the training to go smoothly. I felt a new sense of accomplishment rising inside of me. Over the length of the morning I grew accustomed, comfortable, and confident in each deadly art I'd mastered. The electric pulse running through me powered and intensified the raw ambition.

The last step taken in the muggy, sweat-filled training room, was a quick recap, and technology training. Amber was already familiar with everything reviewed, but for Freddie and I... it was nothing but surreal. We were each handed our own individual tablet, much like the one that never left Judy's grasp. We were taught thoroughly by experts the wonders of technology, by merely the touch of a screen.

Nine

I used my time well in the short journey to the slaughtered village. The hovercraft moved fast, covering ground in a quick enough speed that looking out the windows were not an option. My stomach churned from the movement. I sat as still as possible in my strapped-in position, and tried to hold back an overwhelming motion sickness. I swallowed the rising bile in my throat, convincing myself that Judy was right. She, along with the twenty other men and women that were packed in the craft informed me that it only took a little getting used to, and that the stomach flutters would pass. I hoped they were right as my head and stomach were spinning in opposite directions. I tried to focus my energy on that strange learning device The Company called a tablet.

Judy helped me navigate it. I quickly learned how to tell time first. At a rapid pace, I next studied up on guns, lasers, and bombs of every kind. I was a quick study, as I retained every detail. Not only did I learn of all different types of weapons, but by the end of the flight I could tell you how each weapon was built from the inside out.

I understood the operations of current weaponry in such detail, that I'd even familiarized myself with nicknames and historical uses. Although I'd still never held a firearm, I was now very well acquainted. By the time we reached the village you could put any gun in my hand and I likely would've been able to load, fire, disarm, and disassemble it with ease. My mind was a sponge and I used it as one, soaking up information and absorbing details.

The craft landed softly, and whispers filled the air. We'd arrived at the brutally destroyed village after an hour's flight. I swallowed my pride for the knowledge of exact time, as I unbuckled myself from the seat.

My footing nearly escaped me as I stood. I felt as if we were still moving, and my balance was slightly off. Freddy appeared to have the same troubles with motion, as his body swayed to the sides and his knees buckled upon standing. I chuckled at him under my breath, gained my footing, and joined the line forming by the door.

As we piled out of the craft there were no words. Voices were silenced, as every one of us were rendered speechless. Quiet gasps and heartfelt tears formed in the lips and eyes of everyone. My chest dropped as I took in the scene.

The bodies of the villagers lay lifeless before of me. The Lamian had piled them up together in the center of their huts. One giant stack of death... all skin and bones. Some were chard and burned from The Companies bombs, some were not. Small strands of rising smoke smoldered around them. The smell was unbearable. Dried flesh and burnt hair were rotting in the sun's heat. Flies swarmed, and bacteria collected. Standing out in memory more than any of the others, was the lifeless body of a small boy. I recognized him to be one from the video I'd watched the day before. I recalled his smile and the innocent look in his eyes as he threw a ball to his friends. He was young, a pre-teen at best. I felt Amber's hand slip into mine.

I was unable to take my eyes off the boy, and his protruding eye sockets. The Lamian had sucked him dry. His cheeks were deflated, along with his stomach. I could see every bone in his hollowed body. He'd been tossed aside on the top of the pile. I had to make myself look away. I allowed my eyes to scan the rest of the faces. A permanent fear was petrified into their eyes, and each of their mouths were open. I could tell by the look on their dead faces, that they had been taken by surprise. Their lives taken brutally and unexpectedly.

The sound of a puking Company man chimed in directly behind me. His stomach was apparently unable to handle the situation, as were several others as they gagged and choked down the similar notion. I held my shaking hand over my nose and mouth in an unsuccessful attempt to block out the scent.

Major Kingston stepped out of the craft last. I watched him close as he pushed past us. He turned his back to the hideous display, facing the crowd. His face remained stern and unreadable. I was unable to tell if he was a heartless and unemotional man, or if he was actually the strongest I'd ever met. I mirrored his expression and squared my shoulders.

He spoke loudly, demanding attention and respect. Everyone aside from Judy and Brock, froze in place and listened to him. Judy hung her head in sorrow and drug her feet slowly back into the hover craft. She was quietly followed by Brock, tears flowed freely down each of their faces. They disappeared back into the hidden comfort of the craft in wait to be returned to the safety of The Company walls. This was clearly not a place for anyone with too kind of heart, or too weak of stomach.

"We don't have time to bury them now. Another craft will be coming with men that will take care of them. The day is shortening. We still need to set up camp, and our soldiers need food and rest. We're going to have a long night. Everyone needs to split up and look for any kind of clues that may help us in anyway. We had crafts out all day yesterday, and this morning, while you were all in training. They were looking for sign as to what direction she went and were she might be hiding out. So far, they haven't been able to find anything. We must know *something* in order to set camp in a reasonable place.

"We want her to fall for our decoy. We want to stop her before she reaches The Company. If she gets there first, then we're praying the wall will hold her out. At least until you all can get there to fight her. Every option we have right now is a long shot, so this is our chance. This is our opening to stop a Lamian and learn her strengths and weaknesses. Because we don't know how many are out there, we start here."

The group dispersed and fanned out in every direction. Amber and I walked hand in hand through the village remains. Smoke was raising from their huts that were burned to the ground by The Company. Random mud clumps and charred sticks were all that remained. It was nearly impossible to tell where one hut may have stood, or where one landed from the blasts. The unbearable smell lingered in the air, leaving an imprint of rot in my nostrils and the taste of death in my mouth.

It was hard to swallow, and my eyes were burning. The heightened senses made our task much harder than the military men around us. A new and true understanding of death clung in the back of my mind as we walked around the smoldering village. I thought about the kids playing ball, so free and careless, only to be ripped from their homes and slaughtered in the middle of the night. I'd been looking forward to the fresh air beyond The Company walls, yet at that very moment I wanted nothing more than to climb back into the hovercraft and be zipped back to the safety of it.

"Is this really what the world is like?" Amber asked. "These people had nothing, and now they are dead."

Her observation hit home. I'd been thinking about the way they'd died, and not the way they'd lived. Apparently, her mind was stuck in a different setting. My life was similar to theirs, but I was happy. I'd never known of The Company's lifestyle, nor had I cared to. My father and my cave had been my entire life. It was a life without the burden of other people's habits or opinions. A life full of love and simplicity.

Until being taken from my home I knew nothing of war, stress, agenda, or politics. I'd grown up without the convenience and luxuries of The Company, yet I always considered myself lucky for it.

"These people had everything." I said. "They had family and love, they were happy. They were innocence in its purest form, and this was home. It's all they'd ever known. You can't miss out on things that you don't even know exist."

As I said the words, I realized that I was talking about myself just as much as the people of this village. I fought back the tears that'd been continuously rising since I stepped out of the craft. My fingers tightened around hers as I thought of my father. God, did I ever miss him.

"Is this really how you lived?"

"Yes and no." I tried to explain in a way that she could understand. "I lived in a much prettier place with plant life, water, and animals. My home is very different from this place when it comes to surroundings, but if you're talking about possessions, then yes. I lived like these people. I didn't have much, aside from my cave and my father. But I didn't need anything else. I was happy at home. I never wanted anything more, and I'd give anything now to get it back."

My voice cracked, but I held my head high. I knew exactly who I was, and I was proud of that man. The dead people of this village wouldn't want a crying child here to avenge them. They'd want someone who was strong and confident. I was determined to be that man, and I knew that Amber and Freddy were too. The dead deserved that much. I swallowed my sorrows, not allowing the tears to escape.

"What is that?" Amber interrupted.

"What?"

"There." She pointed into the sand hills.

We were walking around the outer edge of the burned huts. Sand, and swells of more sand, was stretched across the horizon. It was apparent that the powerfully blowing wind had covered up any tracks that the Lamian may have left behind. Amber pointed far beyond the village towards the falling sun.

"Can't you see that? Something is shining out there. Come on."

It was far away in the hills. Much farther than the average human sight could've seen. Freddy must have been channeling in on our conversation because he responded almost instantly.

"I'm right behind you, Jack." He hollered.

His voice was calm and collected, as it sounded from across a few burned huts. I could hear each and every man talking as they walked around the remains, but for some reason Freddy's voice stuck out in my ears.

The object caught the sun at just the right angle giving us a perfect view, from what could easily have possibly been miles away. As Amber and I took off in a speedy walk Freddie was soon at our side. With the straps of two large Company bags tossed over his shoulders, and one in his hand.

"That refection is very far away, there's no time to waste." He exclaimed, as he tossed Amber a bag freeing up his arms. The other two remained on his shoulders as he continued. "I watched the military men pack dozens of these bags with our weapons, while we were supposed to be learning of electronics." He rolled his eyes in disgust at The Companies stupidity. "They should've been showing us more important things, like our baggage and blades, than stupid stuff that we have no immediate need for." Freddie had proven himself to be wiser than The Company yet again.

"Anyway, I swiped them from inside the craft doors on my way through the village. I've had my eyes on them, and on the Major since we landed. We should always keep ourselves armed, even if The Company men aren't smart enough to do so. Let's get ourselves situated and then, we run. We may need to be ready for a fight when we get out there. I'm sure the military men and the Major won't be too far behind us as soon as they notice us moving. But we must get there first. We don't want them causing problems or getting in our way."

"Don't you think we might need their help?" I interjected.

"It's possible, but my guess is that they'll be more of a burden than help. I don't know about you, but I'm willing to take my chances without them."

I agreed with his logic. "We'd better do this quickly then, and get to whatever's out there before they can stop us. Give me that bag." I said, as he tossed me the second one.

We opened the bags as quickly as possible, knowing that we'd be noticed in a matter of seconds. We had no time to spare or waste as we rushed into preparation. A nagging realization harped in the back of my mind that the

Major had to have been on the phone with The Company men listening in, right at that exact moment. We had no secrets. We each pulled apart our own pack and strapped on our gear, hurried yet precise.

Each blade was wrapped, holstered and ready to be strapped on. The long cold blades were placed at our waists. Deadly axes were secured in the shape of an X across our backs, allowing them to be easily accessed. Taking only a mere amount of moments Freddie, Amber, and I had our weapons in place, secured, and were ready to fight. As I quickly fastened the last strap of the well packed and assembled knife vest around my chest, the sound of the Majors voice cut through me. He pointed in our direction and shouted at the men to stop us.

"Let's go, now!" Amber shouted.

Taking off in a sprint, we began running in the sand. Though the texture of the earth was so much different than the dirt outside my cave, it was still a welcomed run. The air was crisp as we escaped the awful smell of death in the village. We were fast. Much faster than the military men behind us. I glanced over my shoulder at the gap between us as it grew larger and larger. My heart sped with adrenalin and my breath remained steady. It was exhilarating. With Freddie and Amber at my sides, we held the same pace. Faster and faster we ran through the sand. Up and down each swell our feet carried us towards the shinning object in the late afternoon sun.

We ran away from the control of The Company and toward the unknown dangers that lurked ahead. The same fearful energy that pulsed through my veins upon wakening from the injection returned. What lay ahead could be the death of any of us, yet we not only faced it, but ran to it in full force. Flashes of the Lamian ran through my mind and my heart skipped a beat. Images of my afraid and scrambling father pushed me forward. The face of the lifeless boy from the village filled me with vengeance, as I pushed faster over the sandy earth. Even the thought of Freddie's scar flashed in my mind. *This is it*, I thought. *This is your chance to prove yourself and be the man your father taught you to be.* Amber's exact phrase came to mind, "How do we kill this bitch?"

I reached behind my back to clutch the handle of an axe, as we grew closer to the shinning object. Though I was still unable to tell exactly what the object may be, the shine grew bigger. Next to it was a dark spot in the sand. We began to slow to a much more cautious jog as we approached. The military men were very far behind us, and clearly winded as they struggled to catch up. We'd closed the gap between the village and the shinning object in the sand in a matter of minutes. We had plenty of time to investigate before we would be joined by The Company forces.

"I still can't tell what it is." I observed, in a very low whisper.

"Me neither." Amber squinted and strained her eyes towards it.

"I've seen this before." Freddie stopped his stride and crouched down. We followed his lead and bent at the knees next to him. Our conversation was held as quietly as possible. "Not the reflection, but the black hole. Remember how I told you about escaping the creature?"

"Yes." Amber and I answered his question in unison.

"The creature is in that hole. She may not be far, so we can't get any closer than this." He paused. "For now, anyway."

"Are you sure?" I asked. "How do you know this?"

"They burrow those holes underground. That's where they hide out to rest between feedings. My family and I found one just like this, a few miles from my home. My mother went in first. It was an entire morning before she came back out. She said that the hole stretched underground for miles, surfacing now and then in hidden places."

"That must be why The Company can never see them from the hovercrafts during the day." Amber said.

"Yes. We were standing by the entrance talking about the strangeness of it all when it happened. The serpent was fast, and big. My mother must've woken her while inside the hole. She grabbed my mother and sister first, pulling them back into the hole. It took only seconds for the screaming to stop. She moved as if in flashes. My little brother was next. She popped out, and then pulled him back in, disappearing into the darkness."

"I thought The Company said that they only move and attack at night?" Amber asked.

"I wonder if that's why she only came out of the hole for seconds at a time." I joined. "Do you think they're affected by the day light?"

"Yes." Answered Freddie, without missing a beat. "I thought about this while they were teaching us of the beast back at The Company. I remembered the way that she moved in and out of the hole, only grabbing who was closest. It was like she couldn't see us in the light. My older brother and I were standing together the furthest away. As it took my youngest brother next, we both turned to run. It all happened so fast. I was two steps ahead of my oldest brother when she grabbed him, swinging at me in the process. I pushed myself forward, barley out of her reach. One of her claws caught me just under my jaw line next to my ear. The skin tore from my body as I got away. And then I heard it. Along with the yell from my brother as she took him back into the hole, her scream was unforgettable. It was the loudest and highest in pitch sound I've ever heard. It carried across the beach and echoed in the waves of the ocean next to me."

"Oh my God." Whispered Amber. "What happened?"

"My brother stabbed her. He was a great hunter. He was always the fastest of all my family. My brother was a skilled man with a knife, and fearless. I always looked up to him. I still look up to him."

"Did he kill her?" I asked, completely engrossed in his quiet tale.

"Yes. The screams lasted for several minutes. I stopped, dead in my tracks, frozen. I was afraid to move or to try and help him. I listened to the strange creature screaming and whaling until all the sudden it stopped. Everything was quiet. I didn't know what to do until I heard a faint cry for help. My brothers voice was hardly a whisper. I ran back to him. I was lightheaded and hardly able to move myself, as the blood poured out of my neck."

"Oh my God." Amber repeated. I noted the wide-eyed expression on her face.

"My brother was laying across the scales of the beast, just inside the opening of the hole. His body was motionless as he gasped for air. He'd stabbed her several times in the neck and chest all while she squeezed the life out of him. I collapsed over her giant scales next to my brother. I could hardly keep my eyes open and had lost feeling in my legs and arms. I watched him take his last breath before I blacked out. I'm lucky to be alive. My father heard the screams and ran to our aid. He pulled me away from the scene and patched me up. It took him weeks to nurse me back to health. My father, my sister, and I are now all that remain of our family."

The sound of the slow running footsteps of The Company men were approaching. "Hurry." Freddie whispered. "We have to go back and stop them from coming any closer. If she is on this end of the hole we don't want them to wake her. We need to make a plan and prepare."

The three of us slowly stood, peaking over the hill we'd stopped at. We investigated the large swell ahead of us, containing the hole. I squinted my eyes in the sun to make out the shinning object. Catching the light at just the right angle laid a long, perfectly chiseled rock dagger. My eyes widened, as did Amber's and Freddy's. There were no such rocks around to make a weapon like this. It had to have traveled and ended up into the hands of one of the village men. It sat in a giant puddle of blood. The color of the rock was exactly the sort that could be found in my own village. I'd made weapons almost exactly like this one with my father. It is the same type I'd used all my life to hunt with.

"Freddie, what kind of knife did your brother use to stab the Lamian he killed?" I whispered.

"Rock. Just like that one."

His quiet answer was flat and emotionless.

"I'm going to get it. If The Company's right about the materials of our weapons then we might need it."

"Your right." Amber whispered. "Especially since there's no time or material to make more by tonight. How are we going to get it?"

Without second thought or hesitation I took off in a sprint towards the rock spear and the eerie black hole. I doubled my speed as I ran down hill to the bottom of the deep sand swell, and then headed back up the other side toward it. I grabbed the bloody weapon in one quick movement and turned my sprint back towards Freddie and Amber. The blood on the spear was wet, fresh. The scent was foreign. It was a rotten, and very potent smell.

The black hole remained silent and I dared not turn around to look. I didn't even want to know if she was behind me, I was determined to out run her if that was the case. Freddie was right. We needed to make a plan, and to be prepared for a fight whenever possible. As I reached him and Amber, they were bent at the knee, crouched over, and ready to join my side in the run.

We closed the gap between the hole and the approaching military men quickly. We reached the closest few stragglers first, they were only a few yards away. They must've been in the best shape, because they were much closer to us than the rest. We continued to run directly past them without stopping. They shouted and cussed as we passed them, again unable to reach out and catch us. We were far too fast. Normally, I would've been amused at such a circumstance, but with the shock from my closeness to the cave, and with the bloody spear in my hand I had no time for humor.

The words of Freddy's story were bouncing around my head, as we ran for our lives away from the grounds' hollowed out burrow. Freddie had still only spoken to me and Amber, refusing to address or waste his time with a Company man. I shouted over my shoulder at them.

"Turn around! Run fast too, you don't want to be alone out here!"

For a second, I watched their faces over my shoulder. There looks turned from anger, to confusion and fear. They all turned on their heels and began to jog back in the direction of the village.

We passed the next group of winded and worn out men in the same manner. We continued our speedy pace until we were again engulfed in the smell of dead bodies in the village. We ran straight to the Major. We stopped in front of him and stood at attention. I clutched the spear with a tight grasp feeling the strangely scented fresh blood stick to my fingertips.

Though fear was boiling in my veins, the run was needed. It left me feeling refreshed and energized. It helped me swallow my fears and stay focused. Though it had tired the rest of the men, it had only calmed my growing nerves. I can only assume that Amber and Freddie felt the same way. By the looks on their faces, and reassurance in their composure, my assumption was proven to be correct.

I looked at Freddie in question before addressing Major Kingston myself. Freddie shot a look at the Major, and then shook his head at me. I understood his unwillingness to comply with Company personnel. I too had been taken away from everything I loved. I admired Freddie's stubbornness. Freddie looked away from us all, allowing me to do the talking. As I opened my mouth to explain, the Major held up his hand to silence me.

"We wait for the rest of the men." His order was stern, as was the furrow in his bushy brows. "I've been given instructions, Jack. You three have free reign from here on out. You'll be addressing the men. Not me."

Major Kingston pursed his lips in anger. He paid no attention to the new and bloodied weapon I held. He stood tall and was clearly upset at our display of defiance, not realizing that we may have just saved the lives of every man there. He was stubborn, and too blind to note the obvious.

Ten

I glanced at the Major's watch as we stood in wait for the rest of the men to join us. It took nearly twenty minutes for them all to arrive back at the village. Huffing and puffing, they were all completely out of breath. Most were hunched over grabbing their knees. The remainder gagged and coughed, as the smell of the rotting bodies choked off their throats. They took in deep gasps, struggling for oxygen. I couldn't help but to feel superior. They were physically weak in comparison, every last one of them. In a strange way I was sorry for them.

A strong sense of leadership swept over me. I could feel it in the depths of my heart, and the pit of my stomach, that the lives of these men and women depended on me. I felt as if I was looking from a distance into the situation, rather than looking out as a part of it. I was aside and above myself. Freddie was strong and wise, but he was stubborn and unwilling to step up to the task. Amber had a temper and would quite possibly loose it if questioned.

The Major had clearly been in control up until this point, but he was also too self-absorbed to asses' critical situations properly. This left only me to step up and assume responsibility for the lives of these men and women. I allowed my eyes to scan the faces of the tired crew, my crew. Red in pigment with beads of sweat, they looked young, tired, and scared.

This was the first time I truly noticed them. The realization hit me like a punch to the face as I stood strong. I held a bloody dagger that had clearly penetrated the Lamian we were meant to kill. I was growing in ability and sureness. They were weak and full of doubt. I was a hunter, and they were sheltered from the world. Even with all their training, they were clueless and unprepared in comparison. They were forced by The Company to fight, just like me.

They each had a story to tell just like Amber, Freddie, and I. It didn't matter that they'd been trained to fight or that they were familiar with the blade. They'd never been in real combat. Not one of these military men or women had taken a life. Whether it be a human or animal life they were innocent in the art of killing. I was surrounded with fresh faces, eager to learn, yet afraid to use the skills they'd been taught. Freddie had been right. The Company lucked out finding him and I, at least we were hunters. These military folks were ignorant.

I looked into the pleading eyes of a young man that was standing closest to me. I studied the selfish anger that was written all over Major Kingston. Just as he opened his mouth to shout commands, I stepped forward. He closed his mouth quickly, as per his orders, and looked at me with a hint of speculation. I straightened my back, held my head high, and stood at the Major's side as his equal. His stern looks melted, as he relaxed his brows and listened intently for what was to come. It seemed like my brave notion intrigued him, as well as the rest of the group. I addressed them in confidence, absorbed their proud energy, and used it as I spoke.

"I'm a hunter. My entire life has been spent as a predator." I began loudly.

I gripped the rock dagger tightly in my fingers. I gazed into their eyes as I spoke, holding their attention. For the first time I *wanted* The Company to see what I was seeing and hear what I was saying. Up until this point, the mission was full of confusion. It was a fearful scramble. I meant to bring order, strength, and determination to the crusade. I chose my words wisely, for I knew our lives depended on it and our time was running short.

"Since this morning, I've trained and flown with you, and I've been too selfish to get to know you. But I do know this; you're strong and you've taught us well. We're all here for a reason. Our purpose is simple. We are to hunt! And, we are here to kill!"

I held the dagger high, so that every man and woman in front of me could see the blood and feed off my words.

"From this point on I won't let myself be scared, and neither will you. *We*, as hunters, have no room for that." I pulled my father's strength from deep inside of me. I pointed the dagger towards Freddy and continued. "This man has seen a Lamian killed. As a man ready to fight, that gives me hope! I know that if one man can take this creature down, then as a group, we can too! I hold in my hand a weapon that has already penetrated the very serpent that we are here to eliminate."

Eyes widened, and mouths dropped.

"She may be miles away underground, and she may or may not be wounded. She could also be close to this entrance and healthy, ready to surface at any moment. We cannot tell these things, and it's too risky to go in and find her. We must follow a plan and wait for her to find us. I promise you all, that if you only trust Freddy, Amber and myself rather than working against us, then our odds of survival are great. You cannot question our judgment or step ahead putting yourself at risk."

My voice rose louder and more determined, as the anger and purpose filled up inside of me.

"The Company may be forcing us to fight. They may be using our strengths for their own advantage."

I knew there'd be repercussion for my words, but at the very moment I didn't care. The Company needed to hear it, the men needed to hear it. And, possibly most importantly… I needed to say it.

"But, they're also hiding behind the wall like cowards! Right now, that doesn't matter. Right now, nothing matters except for the fact that we are here!" I shouted the last words.

Nods and grunts of approval began rising from the crowd. I continued my loudly voiced opinion, motivating the men and women, giving them exactly what they needed to carry on the journey.

"Out here we don't have a wall to hide behind! We have each other! And we have this!" Again, I held the dagger high. "We'll hunt this serpent down, and we'll kill her proudly!"

The crowd roared. I looked out into their faces at their new-found courage. That very moment was my reason. It finally made sense to me, why I had to be the one containing the G-Factor. I was strong, and I was meant to lead. My entire life I was sheltered, yet I'd been groomed for this very day. My father taught me to be the man who was meant to lead human kind into victory. My chest pounded with eager anticipation and pride.

I knew that The Company would forever be an unwelcome part of me and for the first time, I didn't care. I was in the moment, and the moment was telling me to survive. It was telling me to lead these people, so that they could live on to see their families. I would see my father again someday, I just knew it, and he would again be proud to call me his son. I was becoming a warrior by force, and I was strong enough to find an acceptance of it. I was more powerful because of it. With the help of this group we could kill this Lamian, as well as many more to come, of that I was sure.

The men and women shouted their hurray's. They whopped and hollered loudly for the victory that was to come. Standing as an equal to Major Kingston felt good. No words can explain what I felt inside as I peered out at our small but determined army. I turned my attention to the Major allowing him to take his turn with the eager crew. He stood tall at my side.

The light in his eyes told me that he too may have had a change of heart. He knew that we were in this together. From that moment on, we would be included in all decisions. Our input would be considered and respected. We'd have the freedom to come and go as we pleased… to a point. We were officially in the game that was The Company. I, ready to play.

We'd earned this form of trust and lenience. Though I'd eventually reap the reproductions of calling The Company men cowards, timing was impeccable. They couldn't afford to compromise the mission. My punishment wouldn't come until our return to the city. After a short instruction from the Major we all made out way back into the craft.

I resumed my place next to the distraught Judy. She informed me that she and Brock had spoken to our Company superiors, and that the two of them would be returning to the Third Division tonight. She wouldn't be joining us for the remainder of the crusade. I was on my own. She'd remain out of harm's way, and for that I was thankful. As the last few men were strapped into their seats, the hovercraft lifted.

The movement dropped my stomach and left me to feel nauseated yet again. Judy handed me a small leather pouch containing the tiny sleeping pills to aid my racing body into relaxation. Along with the pills, was a written mathematical table explaining how many pills to take for the exact amount of time to sleep. I looked over the note and then handed it back to her. I'd memorized it that quickly and had no need to carry it around. I slipped the pouch into my pocket, and I thanked her for everything she'd done for me.

"You be careful, Jackson Bellony, and you take care of that beautiful young lady over there."

I took a long look at Amber. Brock had also given her a similar pouch and instructions, but their goodbyes were much less heartfelt than that of mine and Judy's. I figured that she was listening to my conversation with Judy though her face remained unreadable. She was indescribably gorgeous as she sat in her seat without emotion. She was completely stone faced.

"Trust me Judy, I plan on it." I replied as my eyes continued to stare at Amber's profile.

The Major had taken his seat, directly on the opposite side of me and Judy. He waited patiently for me to finish my goodbyes with her, before we continued to plan.

"That hole the Lamian made was between the village and The Company. I think it is safe to say that she's headed in that direction, just as we'd assumed."

"Yes sir. Freddy said that the last Lamian's dugout he saw stretched for miles. I think we'll be better off setting camp rather close to The Company walls. Maybe only a few miles away. If she already has her sights set on The Company, then we don't want her to pass up our camp without smelling us there."

"Yes, your right." The Major pressed a button on a device in his hand and shouted orders and coordinates to the Captain of the Hovercraft.

"Now, let's just pray that she reaches us first."

"Well, even if she doesn't, we'll be close to The Company walls. We can make it there to fight her quickly. Hopefully before she can find a way in. How far underground is The Company wall anchored?" I asked. "If she is moving underground, then it may not be much of a struggle to burrow beneath the wall, and not surface until she is already inside."

"The wall is secured in place with concrete for a half a mile down. Our power source is directly beneath that. There isn't much space to squeeze between, before coming back up into the soil. It was built that way to prevent people from digging their way inside. It should be far enough underground to at least slow her down, if nothing else. Let's hope, anyway."

"Yes, let's hope." I agreed.

I glanced over at Freddy who gave me a nod of approval. He still refused to speak with the Major. He looked directly at me, ignoring Major Kingston's presence completely.

"The plan sounds okay. I'm assuming you used traps to help catch the prey you hunted back home?" Freddy's look was serious, and his voice was deep as he spoke to me from across the craft. "Hidden traps and camouflage were the only things I could think of that'll come in useful that was not covered in our training this morning."

"Yes, I did." I jumped in with a slight excitement. "My father and I would use traps all the time, mostly snares."

"Well, I know that The Company uses nets." He paused to flash the Major a long and hard glare before continuing. The Major held Freddy's glare with an apologetic expression and then looked away. Freddy turned his attention back to me. "I don't think their net guns are big enough or strong enough to hold the Lamian back, or even to slow her down for that matter, but there's got to be some way we can use them. If nothing else, but to give us some warning that she is coming before she reaches us."

I thought hard about it. "What if we tie them together? We could make a few trip wires to trigger them outside of our camp."

"Yes." Answered Freddy. "That might actually work to buy us some time."

"It is getting late, and you'll only have a few hours to rest before the sun is down." The Major again joined our plot. "My men and I can handle this, and we can set up camp while you sleep."

He pulled a bag out from under his seat. He reached into it and pulled out three tiny plastic ones, marked with symbols of food. They were each only a few inches long and about a foot wide.

"This should be enough food to hold your stomachs until the morning. You'll need to rest as soon as we land. The men will set up your tents first. We'll set up the rest of the camp, eat ourselves, and build these net traps and trip wires while the three of you rest."

The Major handed Freddy and me each a food pouch, and then tossed the third to Amber. She sat on the other end of the craft, listening in quietly. She had taken that seat to be next to her nurse, and to gather her thoughts during the flight. She clearly needed a few quiet minutes to herself. I'd given her the space she needed and taken my seat next to Judy without question. I watched Amber turn as the food pouch was tossed, and she caught it with ease. She tore the corner off and began sucking the contents without a word. She continued to stare off blankly, as she slurped down the food pouch.

Freddy and I followed her lead and peeled off a small corner of plastic. I hesitated as I put the pouch to my lips. It wreaked of onions and rotten potatoes. I slowly placed it on my bottom lip and began to slurp it down as Amber was. A thick gel made its way slowly through my mouth and down my throat. The smell was disgusting but the taste was bearable. There wasn't much to the texture, it was a bit slimy. I was pleasantly surprised as the flavor rotated from that of a banana to that of a ripened pineapple.

Just as our food pouches were finished, the hovercraft touched ground. It was a little bit easier to gain my footing this time around. I unstrapped myself and joined the line forming to exit. I moved with the determined crew as we again stepped out onto the sand. I took in a deep breath. The air was much cleaner than the last time we'd completed a flight, and it was refreshing. Amber, Freddy, and I, opted to go for one quick run as the crew set up our tents. I wasn't quite sure what to expect out of a tent.

I'd never heard the expression before. I decided to wait and see exactly what it was myself, rather than asking. We had more important things to worry about. I watched closely as a second and much smaller hovercraft landed. Within seconds, it gathered Judy and Brock and lifted back into the air. Zipping away with incredible speed.

We ran together as a team, circling the hovercraft within a half of mile's distance. We looked out into the sand swells. There was a bit more cactus and brushes than there had been by the village. I even saw a rabbit take off into the hills. We canvassed the area looking for anything that may appear out of the ordinary, but there was nothing. I pictured another Lamian hole in my mind's eye and was slightly disappointed when we didn't see one. I guess I had my hopes up on an easier mission than what may lay ahead. By the time we made two complete circles around the craft our tents were set, and our bedding was in place.

The tents were made of light brown canvas matching the sand around us in color. They were held up and in place by plastic sticks. There was one large tent in the center of camp. It was surrounded by Company men, setting up smaller tents around it in a circular pattern. We were joined by a sizable Company man who introduced himself as Kale.

He explained to us that by placing us in the center, we should be able to hear everything going on around us. We'd be the most protected against the Lamian as she first arrives, allowing us to know she is coming. This would hopefully give us time to prepare for the fight. We wouldn't experience as intense of an ambush, as we may encounter if placed on the outside edge of the camp. The logic made sense, but saddened me. I knew that the military men on the outside edge of camp were possibly volunteering their own lives for the cause.

We thanked Kale sincerely. The three of us stood in the center of our tent watching his exit. I pulled the pouch of pills that Judy gave me out of my pocket, let out a long surrendering sigh and downed the hatch. I collapsed onto The Company cot that was closest to me and let my mind slip into a vast darkness.

Eleven

We'd been in camp for exactly three days. The Company sent out water and food every day, yet it was still sparse and very well rationed. The days were hot, and the nights were long. Though it didn't seem so at the time, looking back now, the first twenty-four hours in camp were actually quite comical. The Military men and women would jump, wake up, reach for their weapons or even scream in fear with the sound of the lightning and thunder.

The next day they were completely exhausted from lack of sleep. This played out well on their part. They were quickly able to change their sleep schedule and stay awake at night, alongside us. After the first disturbing night, they were able to adjust and sleep in the quiet, and safety of the day. Freddy and I felt perfectly at home with the lightning. We may've been on edge in anticipation of the Lamian, but we both remained completely un-fazed by Gods hand striking down from the sky. It had the exact opposite effect on us as it did the crew. It was comforting and reminded us both of the life we'd lived before The Company had taken us from it.

The very first strike of lightning on the very first night in camp had taken Amber's breath away. Everyone else from The Company were in their tents attempting to rest. Amber on the other hand, was out in the open with Freddy and me. We were standing just outside of our centralized tent. I can still see the gap form between her lips, and the spark light in her eyes.

Her body never flinched at the crash of the following thunder. She remained steady and completely mesmerized.

"Beautiful." She whispered.

I was equally transfixed, but not by the sky or earth in reaction. I was unable to take my eyes off her. The way her hair fell across her face in the light of the storm, and the way she grinned with every crash, was intoxicating. I was absolutely bewitched. I stood beside myself, in a trance as I watched her. Amber, in that very moment, was perfection. I couldn't help myself as I reached over to tuck a loose strand of hair behind her ear. I wanted to see every morsel of her face in the light.

We quickly formed a routine. We ate in shifts and ran the outer circle of the camp, avoiding the trip ropes leading to the hidden nets. We lucked out in dodging the lightning as it crashed around us at night. During the day we slept while The Company men took turns standing guard and resting themselves. By the third night, we were less cautious in wait of the Lamian. We were more prepared for a regular old night just like the previous two. We'd expected her to show up less and less. We couldn't have been more wrong. Amber, Freddy, and I, were all outside the camp running and listening, just as we'd done several times before when it began. Freddy was running an outer circle, about a half a mile further from camp as Amber and I.

The screams came as a shock. They cut into my ears like a serrated knife. My inner drums pounded, and my heart sunk. We'd anticipated her to surface outside of the camp, tripping the nets on her way in. This would've given us a great advantage. Rather than the expected, she burrowed her way above ground, directly in the center of camp.

I remember every detail of that horrifying night. The sounds of death are forever burned into my memory. As we ran to the commotion, the screams grew louder. Lightning crashed about a half a mile away from us. The ground shook under our feet. I felt the electricity of it surge throughout me. I continued to push forward. My fingertips and legs tingled, but I was powered by the screams ahead.

I looked over at Amber as we ran. She pushed forward the same as me, shrugging of the effects of the lightning and its closeness. She shook her arms to her sides as she ran. Freddy was on the other side of camp. He was hidden by the dark of the night.

The camp momentarily lit up with each strike, allowing us to see in flashes where we were going and what lay ahead. Screams of pain and confusion were coming from all directions in camp. It seemed she was everywhere. I remembered Freddy's exclamation of the Lamian's scream when we'd first found her hole. I briefly wondered in my quick run why I hadn't heard it yet. Were the men not fighting her? Amber and I hurdled a trip wire in unison, being sure not to set it off as we ran. Gaining ground and increasing in speed we made our way between the first few sets of tents. A few men ran past us in the opposite direction. They were fleeing. With weapons in hand they were not fighting, but scattering the wrong way.

Another flash of light, and there she was. She was still far away and out of reach, but she was apparent. Her long, thick shinning scales were wrapped, circled, and intertwined throughout the tents. consuming more than half of the camp. The top of her head stuck out just above the largest tent... our tent. I'd never seen a head so big. All that I could see at first was her dirty, and matted black hair, her face was still hidden. Just as quickly as the earth around us lit up, it was consumed again by darkness and the air continued to fill with shrieks and terror.

In the next flash we were closing in, yet everything had changed. The serpent portion of her had moved to totally new places. She was quick. Even quicker than I recalled from the videos. Kale, the Military man whom I'd spoken with the most came into view. He was now a lone warrior.

Kale moved by himself closing in on what may have been the center of her serpent half, it was hard to tell in the sudden flash of light. With a blade drawn he sunk it deep into her scales. Again, it was dark. I was expecting a squeal or shriek to escape the creature, but instead an angry hiss echoed around us. As vision came back in another flash, I watched Kale pull his blade back out of the Lamian. Just that quickly, the hole closed up. The healing was nearly instantaneous. Clearly, she'd felt the stab, and clearly she was effected by it.

The tip of her coils suddenly grabbed Kale up and wrapped around him. She spun him in a circle in the air, engulfing him, she effortlessly squeezed the life out of him.

"Freddy, are you close?" Amber yelled as we continued to close the gap.

"I'm just outside of the tents." He yelled back.

"The steal can penetrate her, but it heals instantly." I joined. "It doesn't do any real damage. We have to get to her top half, with the stone dagger. Now!"

Closer and closer we ran, studying and calculating the angles and movements of her serpent half with the brightness of the lightning flashes. She was working her way from the center of camp outward. In speedy flowing movements she was taking the men out. Though her scales would coil the tents and move in strange directions, her entire body as a whole was moving in a clockwise circle. She was engulfing every human life as she made her way through the camp.

As her face and human portion came into view my inner self paralyzed, yet my body continued to run.

The word evil doesn't even begin to describe her. The Lamian's eyes were sharp, and red with a sharpened black line in the center. Her fangs hung low and were stained with blood. Her features were eerie yet intoxicating. Her nose was narrow, and her cheekbones were defined. Her jaw-line was perfectly shaped, that is until she dropped it open to bite. It then stretched and popped out of socket, allowing her mouth to open wider than the length of her face.

Her exposed bodice was chiseled and muscular. She transformed into the serpent half, just below her navel. The scales started out small, then faded into the long fat diamond coils. There was no distinct line where the human-half ended, and the serpent-half began. Her skin was pale with a greenish blue luminosity around it. This must have been her supernatural shield that the military men spoke of. Her filthy black hair was full of dirt and hung long over her shoulders covering her breasts. She moved quickly and with ease, towering over her multiplying victims.

Kale's move was bold, he set an example for the Military men. As Amber and I finished yelling at Freddy, the Majors voice chimed in.

"Attack!" He shouted.

I couldn't see what angle he was coming from, but I could hear him loud and clear over the screams of pain. The men began shouting in unison, yelling their determined and powerful growls of attack. The crew began to jump on the Lamian, stabbing and cutting into her scales. We reached what we assumed to be the center of her serpent half. It was the largest portion in diameter with the biggest scales. Amber shouted at me.

"Go for her heart, Jackson!"

Amber dove on the Lamian. She was fearless. I wanted to stop her, to protect her, and place her out of harm's way, but I couldn't.

Amber sunk a blade deep into the scales but rather than pulling it out she continued to run. The military men stabbed and plunged their weapons into the beast as Amber ran her blade up the center of the beast. She ran on top of the Lamian's scales, hunched over holding the handle to her weapon tightly as she moved. Amber knew that this would only distract, temporarily wound and anger the Lamian. Which was exactly what she was going for, leaving me an opening to inflict a fatal wound. The gap left behind by Amber bled for only a short time before closing back up. It left a damaged red line down the slick, gray and black diamond scales.

The Lamian screeched, hissed and lashed out. She slithered with great force, thrashing herself back and forth. She unsuccessfully tried to shake loose of Amber and the Military men. Curling herself so that her human-half could reach for the crew; she began grabbing, biting, and breaking the men in half with her mighty claws. I was close, so close. Bodies were tossed aside upon being viciously torn apart. The sight and smell of spilled stomach content, and bowels, was overwhelming.

The scent of the Lamians blood was burning my nostrils and watering my eyes. Tents were uprooted and flew into the air from the force of her thrashing. I continued to run. Her screams grew more intense as Amber continued to slice into her. Amber moved with speed and agility on top of the moving scales. She was the ultimate athlete, using the blade as an anchor, as not to be thrown off with the power of the serpent's movements.

As I homed in, closer and closer I tried to quickly calculate my final move-ment. I aimed for one solid and fatal blow. I was a hunter and had been trained to attack intelligently. My father had taught me since I was a small child that you should only *need* to strike once. Whether it be a quick slit of the throat, or an even faster jab to the heart, you may only have one shot… the kill shot.

If you waste your momentum and motion on a bad angle, or with the wrong speed, then the prey will be more likely to get away or strike back before you can kill it. The Lamian was far from prey. She was the ultimate predator, leav-ing me an even smaller a window of opportunity. Thinking fast, I knew that I only had a few seconds before Amber would be torn to shreds by her claws, or drained of blood at the waist by her fangs.

I leapt over the top half of a dismembered body. I used the Lamian's scales as a stepping stone to thrush myself into the air. I jumped with much force and momentum. As I pushed my body forward dagger first, Freddy came into view. He hurled himself into the air at almost the exact same time. He lunged toward her from behind, as I came from the front.

He was two steps ahead, landing on her back, he jabbed his blade into her neck over and over. This caused her to jolt her body backwards, and my dagger to only scratch the surface of her abdomen. I fell unsuccessfully to the ground. Upon landing I curled my body to roll, dodging the edge of the dagger myself.

I jumped to my feet and backed up to get a new run at her. As I looked up at Freddy, I nearly dropped back to the ground in shock. On occasion, I hear the creature whaling in pain as she struggled with him. The look on Freddy's face was heart piercing. I knew deep inside that he was not only fighting her, he was also fighting the previous beast who had taken his family from him. He'd wrapped his arms and legs into her hair, burrowing in, making it harder for her to get a good grip on him. He stabbed her ferociously over and over. Tears streamed down his blood covered face. It was thick running tears, leaving streaks and blotches, mixed in with the maroon colored blood that was seeping from her neck.

I backed up further and further promptly, calculating my run and getting far enough away to gain momentum. I took a quick stock of the crew and my surroundings. Continuous lightning flashes lit the camp. The Lamian thrust her bottom half from side to side. Amber had made it almost halfway up her lengthy scales. She was violently slicing and ripping into the Lamian.

Most of the men were slaughtered. They lay dead around us in bloody pieces. A few had been smashed or sent sailing from her giant movements. The remainder the crew had stepped back, collapsing to their knees in shock as the beast clung to life. They were too scared to run or press forward. It'd been a mere matter of seconds and the destruction was devastating.

I ran back to her, full speed ahead. Blocking everything else out, I focused and concentrated on every step. I watched as she clawed at Freddy slicing into his back, tearing his flesh to pieces as she tried to peel him from her back. She squealed and wrenched with every stab. I again hurled myself into the air using her coiled and bleeding scales to assist my jump in momentum. I pushed myself forward, and with great speed I set my aim for her chest.

Her hair had been flung and matted behind her body with the motion of her arms and Freddy's jabs. She was ultimately exposed. As I pushed toward her, she was finally able to grab a hold of Freddy. Her hand clutched his head and neck crushing his skull. His body limped. Her enlarging jaw dropped exposing her long fangs and split tongue as she prepared for the bite.

Just as she was ready to sink her deadly fangs into Freddy's lifeless body, I reached the center of her pulsing chest. Directly between her breasts I burred the dagger, deep. It penetrated her heart, as the dagger's handle stuck out of her by only inches. Blood dripped down from the wound as she drew in a long, loud, life draining gasp. She dropped Freddy to the ground. Her arms went limp to her side, and her jaw resumed a much smaller and closed position. I too fell to the ground only a couple of feet from Freddy. I was unable to look over at his blood-soaked body. My gaze remained on the dying Lamian.

She gasped for breath and clutched her fatal wound, just before collapsing in a giant heap in front of us. As soon as she was dead I scanned every direction, searching for life, and for Amber. The lightning momentarily stopped. It was a longer pause of darkness than any other throughout the fight. As if the earth and sky were grieving her death, everything became still.

Aside from the short rustle and excruciatingly quiet cries of the few survivors... the quietness consumed me. The smell of her quickly rotting corps began to rise. It engulfed me in the darkness, filling my lungs with rotten humidity, and my mouth with a fresh taste of hot death. I called out for Amber in panic.

"Help!" She whaled in return. "I can't get my leg out! Please, Jackson help me!" Her voice cracked in pain.

I followed it through the dark, thanking God that she was alive. I scrambled to find her location, tripping over body parts in the darkness. The largest and longest lightning bold I'd ever seen crashed just outside the tents. It lit up everything. The power of it shook my body and rang loudly in my ears. It left me deafened and nearly dropped me to the ground. I fell at Amber's side and began pulling her body. Her left foot was trapped beneath the dead weight of the Lamian's serpent-half. Even with our combined strength the task was a struggle.

Working together we were finally able to pull her free. I held her tight. She buried her face into my chest, and she let out a muffled scream of pain. Every bone in her foot and ankle had been crushed. Her foot lay a mashed heap at the bottom of her leg.

"I thought you were dead!" She gasped.

"Freddy didn't make it." I whispered back.

My grip around her tightened as together we caught our breath. Amber composed herself and swallowed the notion to sob.

"What do we do now?" She asked.

"We help the survivors until morning." I spoke as a true warrior.

That night was merely the beginning of my fight. I knew that this was the start of journey, but I didn't realize just how much more struggle and heartache lay ahead of me. The first Lamian I'd killed was a mere stepping stone to the true warrior that I was still molding into. My fate was unfolding. The real war was yet to come.

This Lamian, along with the others in my near future, were hiccups and speed bumps in the much bigger war that was playing out. My life continues to change with every situation that I face. The next challenge was much closer to home than I could have possibly imagined.

About the Author

A SIMPLE LIFE: THROUGH THE EYES OF AN UNEXPECTED AUTHOR.

Growing up in a small town had more than several advantages and disadvantages. Saying that my childhood was sheltered is nothing short of an understatement. Unlocked doors, cleared streets, and the quiet of a trustworthy neighborhood were all welcomed features of my hometown. As a small child I baked cookies with the old lady down the road. I sat next to my kindergarten crush in sun day school, and literally rode my bike in the middle of the road without a care in the world. We didn't have what kids have today. We actually had to use our imaginations to have a good time. There were no smart phones, tablets, or 64s to keep us occupied. We were perfectly content to play with our stick guns and a water hose for hours on end... And I loved it! Along with my scrapes and bruises I also maintained a simple, happy for the little things attitude, and of course a great tan.

Now that I have made my childhood out to be nothing but cherries and smiles, I have to point out the disadvantages that came with the small town upbringing-- before the world of electronics took over the young mind. One word distinctively comes to mind... Boredom! As I grew into adolescence I no longer cared much for silly toys, dancing, baking, or crafts. I rebelled like many young adults do.With a sever chip on my shoulder and a lack of coordination in the sports department, I spent the majority of my time partying. Nothing too outrageous, mostly close friends,fires, and beer.

As much as I would love to say that living in a small town gave me an overactive imagination and love for books, that is unfortunately not the case. I cared more about having a good time than I did about school. I was voted wild child twice in high school. I cheated my way to passing grades.

It wasn't until I was settled and married with a child on the way that I found my love for the literary world. Rearing out of my mid twenties left me a bit more mature, having to find more important things to do with my time than re-occurring nights at the bar. This is when it started - I read one book after another for a few short years, then decided to give writing a bash. I'm completely amazed at the love I developed! Once I started putting the world of imagination that has long been trapped in my overactive mind into a keyboard, the transformation of self began. A new aspiration in life has formed. I want nothing more than to be known as the unexpected novelist who took the literary world by storm!

Books by the Author

Aggravated Momentum
New Age Lamians
Search for Maylee

Lightning Source UK Ltd.
Milton Keynes UK
UKHW041912031120
372650UK00001BB/262